Holy Moses!
(And Other Adventures in Vertical Living)

Also by Bob Hostetler:

They Call Me AWOL

Co-authored with Josh McDowell:

Don't Check Your Brains at the Door

13 Things You Gotta Know
(To Make It as a Christian)

The Love Killer

13 Things You Gotta Know
(To Keep Your Love Life Alive and Well)

Right from Wrong

Truth Slayers

Holy Moses! (And Other Adventures in Vertical Living)

Bob Hostetler

Horizon Books

CAMP HILL, PENNSYLVANIA

Dedicated to
Aubrey and Aaron

Horizon Books
3825 Hartzdale Drive, Camp Hill, PA 17011

ISBN: 0-88965-118-3
LOC Catalog Card Number: 95-77841
© 1995 by Bob Hostetler
All rights reserved
Printed in the United States of America

95   96   97   98   99   5   4   3   2   1

Cover and inside illustrations by Ron Wheeler
Author photo by Stevens Photography, Oxford, Ohio

Contents

The Steps to Vertical Living

The Rewards of Vertical Living

Introduction

*W*hatever you do, don't read this introduction. Introductions to books are always a boring waste of time. And this one is no different. So skip right over this page and dive right into the first chapter.

If you insist on reading these lines, despite the above warning, don't blame anyone but yourself for the consequences. You may fall asleep on the bus while reading this, drop the book into the aisle and ignite a chain of events that results in the end of life on earth as we know it. Just remember, you've been warned.

Even if you don't fall asleep while reading the introduction, this book may put an end to *your* life on earth as you know it. The 31 short chapters of this book, meant to be read in order, may put an end to the frustration and failure you may have experienced in trying to please God and live successfully in His sight. This book may launch you into an experience you never knew was possible, a "vertical" way of living. This book may be the means by which God moves you into a closer, deeper relationship with Him, one in which you participate in the very nature of God Himself (2 Peter 1:4).

If not, keep in mind that it's also perfect for swatting flies and lining small bird cages.

Bob Hostetler

The Need for
Vertical Living

1

Adam's Family

The serpent slithered up to the woman.
"Yo, mama," he said. "Got something for you."

She sighed and rolled her eyes. She knew this snake; he'd once tried to sell her an "authentic" Rolex watch for $15. Another time he offered to take her for a ride in his convertible, but she was too smart for him; she knew snakes couldn't drive.

"Take a look at this," he whispered. His brilliant eyes focused on hers and she stared like a deer caught in headlights. He showed her a shiny emerald-green fruit; the morning dew still glistened on its soft skin.

Her mouth formed a silent "O" at the sight of the food. She had not realized how hungry she

5

had become during a morning of chasing squirrels and making clover necklaces for herself and her mate.

"There's plenty more where this came from," he said, smiling suggestively.

"Where'd you get that?" she said sweetly, and then suddenly she knew the answer. "Where'd you get that?" she repeated, this time accusingly.

"It's tastier than all the fruits in the garden," he told her, locking gazes with her. "It's sweet, and juicy, and tastes warm and cool all at the same time." He pushed the fruit under the woman's nose. "Here, mama, give it a sniff."

"I know where you got that," she said. "You got it from the tree in the middle of the garden."

"So what if I did? Did the Boss Man say you couldn't eat from any of these trees?"

"No," she answered slowly. It seemed like she'd had this same conversation with the serpent many times before, until she could scarcely remember what she'd said, what he'd said, even what God had said.

"We may eat from the trees in the garden," she said, stomping her foot impatiently, "but He did say, 'You must not eat from the tree that is in the middle of the garden, and you must not touch it, or you will die.' "

"Aw, now. You won't die!" The serpent rolled his eyes. "Look here," he said. The serpent suddenly sank his long fangs into the sweet green fruit and swallowed a chunk, smacking and slurping loudly. "Mm mm good," he said.

The woman stared at him like he'd just swallowed his own head.

"Am I dead?" he asked her, smiling.

She studied his sparkling eyes. "No," she said quietly.

"See," he said. He slithered closer to her until his head was almost resting on her shoulder. "The Big Guy doesn't want you eating this fruit because He just wants to control you." He flashed a charming smile. "But *I* think you're old enough to make those decisions yourself, don't you?"

She blinked.

"Of course," he continued, his voice as smooth as dew rolling off a leaf, "I can always eat the whole thing myself."

She stared, unspeaking, at the fruit.

Finally, he jerked the fruit away. "Never mind," he said sharply. "Later, mama."

"No, wait!" she shouted. She covered her mouth with a hand, shocked at the volume of her own voice. "Wait," she repeated, softly. "I want to taste it."

"Now you're talking, mama." He watched with grinning satisfaction as her slender fingers grasped the fruit and lifted it to her mouth. Juice dripped down her chin as she bit into the fruit. Her eyes widened as she chewed, and her face blushed red . . . for the first time. She felt an odd pleasure and something else, something new, something she could not name. She didn't know what to call it, but it scared her. And it hurt.

The serpent smiled. "Now, mama," he said, "let me show you some brand new Gucci bags that I can sell you real cheap."

You know the rest of the story. The woman not only ate the forbidden fruit herself, she offered some to her husband, Adam, and he also violated God's clear—and only—command to the two humans He had created in His image. An angel kicked them out of the garden, and Eve had to raise the original Adam's family in a somewhat rougher neighborhood.

Since that time, of course, we have all been born into Adam's family. Some kids inherit freckles from their parents. Some have red hair because one of their grandparents was a redhead. Some exhibit features and mannerisms that go back for generations! But all of us have inherited the moral characteristics of Adam's family; we come into the world with a natural tendency to sin.

That's why, no matter how hard you try, you can't keep from getting in trouble. That's why, no matter how good your intentions, you can't resist every temptation. That's why, no matter how many times you've determined never to lie or lust again, you can't seem to stop yourself.

Because you are a member of Adam's family, you have an inherited tendency inside you that wants to get mad when you don't get your own way, that leads you to lie, that makes you selfish at times, and proud and impatient and rebellious.

This family trait, which we all share, is much worse than inheriting your father's big nose or your great-aunt Ida's varicose veins; it robs you of the purity and happiness that Adam and Eve once knew. It frustrates you and can even make you feel ugly and hateful in your heart and soul. Most tragically, however, it separates you from God, your Creator, and prevents you from becoming all that He intended.

Bummer, huh? But that's not the end of the story. (Check it out—it's only the first three chapters!) You *are* a member of Adam's family (like the Bible says, "*all* have sinned and fall short of the glory of God" [Romans 3:23]), but you're not stuck. You can't exactly return to the Garden of Eden, but you can reclaim the happiness and fulfillment, the intimacy and intensity of life that you were meant to enjoy. There are a few things you'll need to understand first (and that's what the next few chapters are about), but once you do, you'll be off on an incredible adventure—in "vertical" living.

Word Up

If you want to discover more about your membership in Adam's family and how that membership affects you, take a few moments to complete the following:

- Read Genesis 3:1-24, the account of Eve and Adam's disobedience. Do you think *you* would have acted differently if you had been in Eve's place? Why or why not?

  I probably would have done the same thing Eve did. The devil is very deceiving to us and no matter what kind of Christain you are he can make you sin.

- How would you complete the following phrases? (circle your answers)

  1. Sin entered the world through:
     a. the atmosphere
     b. one man
     c. pods planted by alien spaceships

  2. Death entered the world through:
     a. careless customs inspectors
     b. an open window
     c. sin

  3. Death came to all people because:
     a. all sinned
     b. it spread like a bad rash
     c. it created jobs for thousands of funeral directors

  To find out the correct completions, check Romans 5:12-14.

2

Holy Moses

*H*e blinked his eyes.
"Sun must be baking my brains," he muttered.

The bearded man with the weathered face couldn't believe his eyes. He'd been staring at the sight for several minutes.

He stood on a baked hillside in the harsh, rocky terrain of the desert where he had herded his sheep in an effort to find more grazing land for them. He shook his head and rubbed his eyes with the backs of his dirty, callused hands.

When he opened his eyes again, the thing was still burning.

"No way," he said. The man had been driving his sheep along a stony path when he was arrested by the sight of a scrawny acacia tree. The tree—hardly taller than the man himself— was not unusual; gnarled, thorny acacias dotted the desert. But this tree was in flames.

That was not even unusual by itself. The wildernesses of Midian and Sinai, where he herded sheep, were so dry that plants and trees—almost anything, really—could catch fire easily and be gone a moment later. But this bush was still burning. The flames seemed to lick around the form of the tree and its twisted branches without touching them.

The man lifted a rough hand, reached under his head covering and scratched the top of his head.

"No way," he repeated. He stepped toward the sight.

"Moses!" A voice called his name.

Moses ducked his head as if dodging a low-flying vulture. He looked around frantically but saw no one.

"Moses," the voice repeated.

The voice sounded like it had come from the flaming tree, but Moses had seen a lot of acacia trees in his time, and none of them had ever talked to him. He turned around, and started backing toward the tree as if to defend himself from attack.

"Do not come any closer," the voice said.

Moses whirled once more. The sound had definitely come from the twisted little tree. He suddenly wished he hadn't drunk so much water that morning. He shifted nervously from one foot to the other.

"Take off your sandals," the voice commanded, "for the place where you are standing is holy ground."

Moses looked around at the rugged terrain all around him. *This is holy ground?* he thought. *To whom? Snakes and vultures?* He slipped his sandals off; the sun-scorched sand burned the soles of his feet, and he began hopping from one foot to the other in a grotesque desert dance. He suddenly wished he'd taken that job mining turquoise at Serabit el Khadim.

"I am the God of your father," the voice proclaimed, "the God of Abraham, the God of Isaac and the God of Jacob."

Suddenly, Moses' leathery face turned white, and he threw himself on the ground, covering the back of his head with his hands. He felt sinful and dirty. He began to tremble, and his quavering voice murmured fearful pleas for mercy into the rock and sand of that "holy ground."

God revealed himself to Moses in a burning "bush" in the desert, and Moses' reaction was to fall on his face in fear. Pretty weird, huh?

Actually, it's pretty natural. Moses was an ordinary, sinful guy (he was even a fugitive murderer!) who met up with the awesome, holy God. He discovered firsthand that sinful men and women—even garden-variety sinners like you and me—cannot approach a holy God.

A prophet named Isaiah was worshiping in

the temple in Jerusalem when he met the holy God in a vision. He saw unearthly winged creatures called seraphim and heard them crying back and forth, "Holy, holy, holy, is the Lord of hosts." He felt the walls tremble, and the temple filled with smoke. Isaiah lifted his hands to shield his face, and cried, "Woe is me" (the ancient equivalent of "I'm a dead man!"). He reacted to his encounter with God in much the same way Moses had; he loudly confessed his sinfulness and his unworthiness in the presence of the holy God.

Another guy, whose name was John, met Jesus in a vision. John had been one of the 12 disciples of Jesus; he had attended weddings and funerals with Jesus, he had eaten with Him and slept beside Him, he had taken care of Jesus' mother after Jesus was crucified. Yet when John saw the risen Lord in a vision, he "fell at his feet as though dead" (Revelation 1:17). Though he had been among Jesus' closest friends, he could not stand face to face with the Holy One in His glory.

The men of an ancient town called Beth Shemesh once asked, "Who can stand in the presence of the LORD, this holy God?" (1 Samuel 6:20). Moses once sang, "Who among the gods is like you, O LORD? Who is like you—majestic in holiness, awesome in glory, working wonders?" (Exodus 15:11). "The LORD our God is holy," the psalmist said (Psalm 99:9).

God is holy, and no one—not even Moses

himself—can approach Him or stand before Him, because (as the prophet Habakkuk affirmed to God), "Your eyes are too pure to look on evil; you cannot tolerate wrong" (Habakkuk 1:13).

That, of course, presents a problem. We're all sinners—part of Adam's family, remember—and most of us have sinned more than once (you know who you are). If God is too pure to look on evil, how can we ever hope to please Him? How can we ever expect Him to hear our prayers or help us get through tough times? And how can we possibly expect to stand before Him on judgment day without being condemned?

Tough questions, huh? The answer to them is even tougher: we can't. God is holy, we're not. Adam and Eve blew it way back in the Garden, and we've blown it a time or two ourselves. Sinful men and women can't even approach a holy God; forget trying to please Him. End of story, right?

Not exactly. We just have to find a way to fix our sinfulness, a way to get rid of our "unholiness." Maybe then we can please God. Maybe then He'll hear our prayers and help us through the tough times. Maybe then we can stand before Him on judgment day without being condemned.

It's worth a shot, don't you think?

Word Up

If you want to better understand why our

sinfulness separates us from God and His blessings, take a few moments to complete the following:

- Read Isaiah 6:1-5. Why do you think the seraphs (angels) cried the word "holy" three times to describe God, instead of just once?

  Each time was for the 3 divisions of Christ. The father, the Son. & the holy spirit.

- How did Isaiah respond to God's holiness?

  He cried out to God that he was an unclean man and was ruined now that he had seen God.

- How do you think you would act if you had been in Isaiah's place?

  I think I would have collapsed from shear terror.

- Read Revelation 4:8. How are the heavenly words of praise to God in this verse similar to the cries of the angels in Isaiah 6:3?

  They said the word holy 3 times and the deliverers also had 6 wings.

- How are they different?

  Revelation's talked about the God who was, and is, and is to come. Isaiah just talked about Christ as 3 figures that rained over us.

3

Phil and Jed's Bogus Journey

*I*t felt like a movie . . . a bad movie. Phil and Jed had been abducted by android likenesses of themselves, who took them to a remote area in the desert.

Now, as Phil and Jed climb out of the van to face their android look-alikes, one android announces, "We're totally going to kill you now."

"No way!" Phil and Jed shout in unison.

"Yes way!" the androids answer.

The alien robots wrestle Phil and Jed up the side of a steep, craggy mountain, pose them at the edge of a dangerous precipice and fling them to their deaths on the rocks below.

In the next moment, however, the real Phil and Jed awake and are immediately aware that their bodies feel no pain or injury.

"What happened?" Jed asks.

"Jed, we're dead, dude," Phil answers.

"No way," Jed says.

"Yes way," Phil says, pointing to the lifeless forms of their physical bodies still lying on the rocky desert floor.

Suddenly a black-robed, ashen-faced form appears behind them. Phil and Jed spin and stare, wide-eyed, at the towering figure.

"It's the Grim Reaper, dude," Phil says.

"Oh," Jed says. He turns to the unsmiling apparition. "How's it going, Death?"

The black-robed figure doesn't respond.

"You must come with me," he says, and turns to walk away. He escorts Phil and Jed to the gates of heaven, where they are met by a smiling, white-suited woman who looks like a heavenly flight attendant. She directs them through two glistening white doors that stretch to the height of a skyscraper, and they appear before the throne of God, who is masked from their sight by an intense white light that causes the hapless humans to bow their heads and shield their eyes.

"Dude," Phil says to Jed. "We're in big trouble."

"Hi, God," Jed says, swallowing hard. "I'm Jed. This is Phil."

Phil slaps his friend on the chest. "He already

knows that, dude."

"Oh," Jed says. "Tell Him about all the good things we did back on earth."

"Like what?"

"Like, I don't know. What about that time you stayed home with your sick aunt instead of going cruisin' with me?"

"Uh, dude," Phil whispers, "I lied. I never had a sick aunt. I took Suzanna to the Nervosa concert instead."

"No way!"

"Yes way."

"Oh. Well, then tell Him about the money we collected for the homeless, remember that?"

Phil grips Jed's elbow and hisses into his ear, "Shhh! We spent that money on dirty magazines, remember?"

"Uh yeah. I forgot." He reaches a hand to his head and scratches. "We can tell Him we never killed anybody or robbed a store or anything like that."

"Yeah," Phil answers. They exchange worried glances.

"I know!" Jed says excitedly. "We can promise to be kind to everybody, never do anything wrong and keep our rooms clean for the rest of our lives!"

"Jed," Phil says seriously. "We're dead, dude."

"Oh," Jed says. He squints against the blinding light proceeding from the throne of God. "We're dead, all right."

Phil and Jed's journey is bogus, of course. That is, it's imaginary. But their experience illustrates the predicament we would all be in if we had to stand before the throne of God and gain entrance into heaven by our own righteousness. And even if it were possible for Phil and Jed to get a second chance—if they promised to be kind to everybody, never do anything wrong and keep their rooms clean for the rest of their lives—they could never obtain righteousness through their own efforts.

None of us can do that. No matter how many "good" things we do, we can never become good enough to face a holy God. No matter how many "chances" we get, we will never "make it" in our own strength.

We may try to find acceptance in God's sight by doing good things and trying not to do bad things, but it will never work because "all our righteous acts," the Bible says, "are like filthy rags" (Isaiah 64:6). Trying to erase our many sins with good works is like throwing rose petals into a pig sty; they cannot overcome the stench and will soon be trampled underfoot by the mud and slop we cannot seem to keep out of our lives.

So, as Phil said to Jed, "We're in big trouble." We're all members of Adam's family, unable (because of our sin) to approach a holy God, and we can't erase our sins or obtain righteousness no matter what we try.

So we're stuck, right?

Right. We can't do anything to reverse the effects of Eve and Adam's sin. We're unfit to stand before a holy God, and we can do nothing to make ourselves fit, to achieve lasting happiness, wholeness and holiness. That's the bad news.

The good news? God can do it for us.

Word Up

In order to further explore the predicament of sinful men and women (and that includes all of us), take a few moments to complete the following:

- Each of the following Bible verses refers to one of the effects of sin. Read each verse and then match it with the corresponding effect from the list on the right.

Romans 6:23   Shame
Matthew 13:15   Fear and cowardice
Isaiah 57:20-21   Guilt
Ezra 9:6   Death
Proverbs 28:1   No peace
Psalm 32:5   Spiritual blindness

- If those are truly the effects of sin, why do you think we keep on sinning?

The devil does not give up on us, he keeps at us just as Jesus keeps at us to do wrong.

4

The Problem with Paula's Bed

*P*aula Sue Finkelhaney!" Mrs. Finkelhaney's
shrill voice rang through the house. "Get up
here this minute!"

Paula raced upstairs and saw her mother
standing at the door to Paula's bedroom. Her
mother lifted an arm, like the Ghost of Christmas Future, and pointed into the room, a grim
look on her face.

Paula stepped carefully to the door and
peered cautiously into the room; her mother's
attitude made her half-expect to see a motorcy-
cle gang, dressed in leather and chains,
hunched over her bed playing a game of poker.

Paula could see nothing the matter in her room, however. Everything was just as she left it that morning.

"What's wrong?" she asked her mother.

"What's wrong?" her mother echoed, as if she were the only one who could see the card-playing gang. "Look at that bed!"

Paula looked at her bed in the manner of someone who's just been told a joke she doesn't get. She was beginning to get frustrated.

"What?" she said.

"It's a mess!" her mother answered. She stopped pointing and threw her arms up in a gesture of hopelessness.

"Oh, that? I didn't have time to make it this morning, that's all."

"You didn't have time to make it yesterday either, did you? Or the day before that?"

"I've been busy lately," Paula answered.

Her mother flashed her one of those why-didn't-I-sell-you-to-gypsies-when-I-had-the-chance looks.

"I don't see why I should have to make my bed every day anyway," Paula complained. "It just gets messed up again that night. Make it in the morning, mess it up at night, make it in the morning, mess it up at night. What's the use?"

"Paula Sue, as long as you live in my house, you'll make your bed—do you hear me?" Her arm lifted again in the ghost-of-Christmas gesture.

Paula rolled her eyes, stomped to her bed and began pulling the sheet and cover up.

"I'll just start sleeping on the floor," she muttered. "At least I won't have to do this over and over and over again."

Maybe you've had a similar conversation. Wouldn't it be nice if there were a way to make your bed once and for all, so you wouldn't have to keep doing it morning after morning?

That's sort of what God did in solving the problem posed by our sin. You see, many centuries ago, God provided a way for sinful men and women to once again—as they had in the Garden of Eden—enjoy the fellowship of a holy God and all the blessings He had intended for them, like freedom from guilt and fear of death, like happiness in their lives and wholeness in their hearts.

He did this by instituting a system whereby a person could take a perfect, spotless animal, lay his hands on the animal's head and slaughter the animal as "atonement" for the person's sins. This ritual sacrifice, however, was not performed once, but many times, year after year for as long as a person lived.

That system was imperfect. Like Paula's unmade bed (only at a more profound level, of course), the Old Testament system of animal sacrifices required repetition . . . not because God made a mistake, or couldn't come up with anything better. It was a "preview" of coming attractions, "a shadow of the good things that [were] coming" (Hebrews 10:1).

As the writer of Hebrews said,

> The same sacrifices repeated endlessly year after year [can never] make perfect those who draw near to worship. If it could, would they not have stopped being offered? For the worshipers would have been cleansed once for all, and would no longer have felt guilty for their sins. But those sacrifices are an annual reminder of sins, because it is impossible for the blood of bulls and goats to take away sins. (Hebrews 10:1-4)

All those sacrifices, the perfect, spotless animals that were offered year after year by people wanting to be free from their sin, were signposts pointing the way to the One whom John the Baptist announced, saying, "Look, the Lamb of God, who takes away the sin of the world!" (John 1:29).

God sent His Son, Jesus, to earth to become a once-for-all sacrifice for sins. Jesus lived a sinless life for 33 years, and then gave Himself up to death on a cross. His death met the demands of the Father's justice—because "the wages of sin is death" (Romans 6:23)—and at the same time filled our need for a means of salvation—because "the gift of God is eternal life in Christ Jesus our Lord" (6:23).

By offering Himself as a perfect, spotless, sinless sacrifice for our sin, Jesus eliminated the need for "the same sacrifices repeated endlessly year after year" (Hebrews 10:1). He was the final sacrifice, once and for all, for *your* sin, "because by one sacrifice he has made perfect forever those who are being made holy" (Hebrews 10:14).

You may not be able to make your bed once and for all, but you can obtain forgiveness for and freedom from sin once and for all. If you have not already done so, you can do it now, by sincerely praying a simple prayer like this:

> *God, I am a sinner. I'm sorry for my sins—sorry enough to turn away from them completely. Thank You for sending Jesus to die on a cross for my sins. I accept His sacrifice and on that basis I ask Your forgiveness for my sins.*
>
> *I surrender my life to You and ask You to come into my life through Your Holy Spirit. In the name of Jesus, amen.*

If you have sincerely prayed that prayer, you probably still need to make your bed every morning, but you can rest in the assurance that your sins are forgiven and you are among "those who are being made holy" (Hebrews 10:14).

Word Up

To learn more about Jesus' sacrifice for your sins, complete the following:

- Read Luke 23:33-47. What do you think is the significance of the centurion's statement (in verse 47)? (circle your answer)

    a. It is the reaction of an objective observer to the crucifixion

    b. It testifies to Jesus as a perfect (righteous) sacrifice

    c. It makes a great ending to the story

    d. It has no significance

    e. It shows that even a hardened Roman soldier recognized Jesus as the Messiah

    f. A and E

    g. A and C

    h. A before E except after C

- Read Romans 5:6-11 and complete the following statements:

    "Since we have now been justified by his blood, how much more *Shall we be saved from God's wrath throug him* For if, when we were God's enemies, we were reconciled to him through the death of his Son, how much more, *having been* reconciled, shall we be saved through his life! Not only is this so, but we also rejoice in God through our Lord Jesus Christ, through whom we have now recieved reconciliation."

This really spoke to me because my mom and I had a fight tonight about putting the car away.

5

The Roller-Coaster Ride

*Y*ou plop yourself into the seat and pull the re-straining bar down onto your lap. You turn to your friend who's sitting next to you and flash a smile. Your friend gestures, reminding you to take your ball cap off so you won't lose it in the course of the 50-second ride. You snatch the hat from your head and shove it in your hip pocket.

The car in which you're sitting suddenly jolts forward, and you grip the bar in your lap. The wheels clack on the track below as you and your friend ascend a towering incline that seems to crest in the clouds. After what seems an eternity, your car reaches the top of that man-made mountain, and after a breathless moment at the top of the world, you're sent screaming down a perilous slope at suicidal speed, your stomach clutching at your throat and the muscles in your face stretching your features into a mask of wild and wonderful fright.

The roller coaster propels you down, and up, then around, down, up, down, up, until you arrive back where you began, your breath quick and your heart pounding.

What a thrilling experience! Roller coasters, since the first one appeared at New York's Coney Island in 1884, are the most popular amusement park rides, offering passengers an exciting combination of fright and delight. What is fun at an amusement park, however, is no fun at all in life.

Once you have experienced the forgiveness of sin and new life in Christ, you know that nothing on earth compares to the peace, happiness, fulfillment and excitement that it brings. If you have experienced salvation in Christ, do you remember what it was like? It was like waking up to a fresh life. You felt unspeakably clean, inside and out. You took pleasure in things you had never noticed before, and were moved by things you had previously found empty or boring. You were aware of a bright hope in your heart, a glowing warmth in your soul. You were excited by the things of God, and repulsed at the approach of sin. Your heart was filled with an awareness of God's love for you, and you responded with love for Him and everyone around you. You leaped at the chance to talk about what had happened to you, and you wanted your friends and family to experience what you had.

Before too long, however, you discovered something disturbing. It wasn't just that you came down from the emotional "high" of that initial experience; you came to realize that, while you were definitely different, you were still very vulnerable to temptation. You were "a new creation" (2 Corinthians 5:17), but some of the old "you" remained (Ephesians 4:22, Colossians 3:9).

George Pardington put it this way:

> The first fall took you by surprise. You were not prepared for it. You were cast down, and waves of disappointment broke over your soul. But you took the matter to your Savior. In grief and penitence you told Him all about it. Easily and quickly you found forgiveness and restoration, and then went on your way rejoicing with renewed confidence. But soon the experience was repeated. . . .
>
> You became discouraged. You found your experience uneven and your path crooked. One day you were on the mountain singing, the next you were in the valley sighing. . . . You longed to be pure. But somehow you found that you could not overcome the evil in your life. . . . You promised the Lord that you would not sin, but you could not keep your promise. Will

power was exerted but did not avail. Resolutions were made but broken as often as made. The *love* of sin was gone, but its *power* was not destroyed.*

Such a roller coaster experience, characterized by cycles of sin, repentance and forgiveness, is not only common, it's universal. Every Christian knows what it is like to want to live in victory and constant fellowship with God, only to know repeated failure and frustration in the battle against sin.

In fact, the apostle Paul himself complained about the roller-coaster ride of his early experience. He wrote to his Christian friends in Rome:

> I do not understand what I do. For what I want to do I do not do, but what I hate I do. . . . As it is, it is no longer I myself who do it, but it is sin living in me. I know that nothing good lives in me, that is, in my sinful nature. For I have the desire to do what is good, but I cannot carry it out. . . .
>
> So I find this law at work: When I want to do good, evil is right there with me. For in my inner being I delight in God's law; but I see another law at work in the members of my body, waging war against [me] and making me a prisoner. (Romans 7:15, 17-18, 21-23)

*(From *The Crisis of the Deeper Life*, Christian Publications, Camp Hill, PA, 1991. pp. 37-38)

If that sounds anything like your experience as a Christian—craving victory but suffering defeat, wanting to conquer sin but being conquered instead, striving for purity but never obtaining—then, believe it or not, you are probably right where God wants you! He is able to turn your frustration into fulfillment, your grief into gladness, your despair into delight and your vexation into victory. He knows all about your roller-coaster ride, and He wants to break your up-and-down pattern . . . and put you on top to stay.

He can do all that and more if you'll let Him. All you need to do is begin to live in the vertical.

Word Up

The apostle Paul understood the frustration of a Christian who wants to live a life that is free from sin . . . but can't. See what he said about that dilemma by taking a few moments to complete the following:

- Read Romans 7:18-25. Then respond to Paul's statements by circling the phrase that indicates to what degree the things he says are true of you.

  1. I know that nothing good lives in me

     very   mostly   somewhat   not true
     true   true   true   at all

2. I have the desire to do what is good

    very   mostly   somewhat   not true
    true   true   true   at all

3. But I cannot carry it out

    very   mostly   somewhat   not true
    true   true   true   at all

4. What I do is not the good I want to do; no, the evil I do not want to do—this I keep on doing

    very   mostly   somewhat   not true
    true   true   true   at all

- What does Paul say (in 7:24-25) is the solution to the problem of wanting to do good, to live a righteous, fulfilled life and not being able to do it?

    He tells us to ask God for forgiveness and try to live our lives to the fullest.

6

Living in the Vertical

The old man wrestled his handful of paper and string through the door of his home and closed the door behind him. Large, heavy raindrops splattered around him, and thunder rumbled in the distance. He lifted his face to the sky; a flash of lightning cracked the sky in the distance. He smiled. He walked briskly down the cobbled street and turned into a large grassy area not far from his home.

"Ben! Ben Franklin!"

A voice called his name, and he turned and saw the familiar face of Hugh Cavendish, a baker. He waved an arm at his friend, urging him to catch up while Ben continued walking.

"I can't stop to talk now, Hugh," he shouted to his friend. "I'm out to prove that lightning is electricity." He finally stopped at the edge of a small pond, and wordlessly handed a handful of paper and string to his portly friend, who stood beside him, sweating and panting.

Cavendish watched as his famous friend folded several sheets of paper into a large boat, tied a string to its prow and threaded the string through a metal key.

"What are you doing now, Ben?" Cavendish asked.

"I'm sending this paper boat out onto the water," Ben answered, pushing the vessel onto the choppy surface of the pond. "Then I suppose I'll just hope the lightning strikes my little boat."

Cavendish watched wordlessly as Franklin stood beside the pond, patiently holding the key-laden string as a fisherman holds a pole. Finally, Franklin's friend scratched his head and cleared his throat.

"Uh, Ben? I'm no scientist, but wouldn't it make more sense to . . . I don't know, climb a pole or fly a kite or something if you wanted to get struck by lightning?"

Ben looked at the baker. "A kite?"

"Yeah. You know," he said, pointing to the sky, "the lightning's up there, after all."

"A kite." Franklin looked at the sky and then turned his gaze upon his little paper boat. He scratched his chin. "A kite."

The two men looked at each other for a long moment. Finally, Ben Franklin squinted his eyes, smiled and said, "Nah. Don't be ridiculous, Hugh. A kite!" He turned away from his friend and watched the paper boat bob on the surface of the pond.

We know, of course, that that's not how it really happened. Ben Franklin did use a kite to prove that lightning was a form of electricity; a kite made sense, because Franklin knew that *the direction he had to go, for the power he wanted, was vertical.*

It is no different with you and me. If you want to stop the roller-coaster ride of your Christian life, if you want to achieve victory over temptation, if you want to conquer sin in your life, *the direction you must go for the power you want is vertical.* The key is vertical living.

What is vertical living? Some people call it sanctification, or holiness. Some call it "purity of heart" or "perfect love." Some describe it with the words "constant fellowship" or "the Spirit-filled life." Some say that it's a "second blessing."

Vertical living, however, is simply the spiritual equivalent of what Ben Franklin did with his key on a kite string; it is tapping into the very life of Christ Himself, it is living "in the Spirit," it is walking with God (see Romans 8:9-11).

Buried deep in the pages of the Old Testament are a few short verses about a pioneer in vertical living. His name was Enoch, and his entire biography is recorded in Genesis 5:18-24. Long before the Ten Commandments were given, long before Jesus was born and died and resurrected, long before the Holy Spirit was sent to dwell in people's hearts, Enoch "walked with God" (Genesis 5:24).

How did he do it? He lived "in the vertical." He certainly must have known that there were obstacles to vertical living. The world was wicked then, as it is now. And Enoch had no Bible, no Christian books, no Christian music, no church youth group. In fact, by the time his great-grandson grew up, the world had become so filled with sin that God destroyed it with a flood, sparing only Enoch's great-grandson and his family.

But Enoch did not let the obstacles prevent him from walking with God; he determined to take the necessary steps to vertical living. Like Ben Franklin flying a kite instead of floating a boat, Enoch apparently knew (or discovered) that the proper direction to go for the power to live righteously was vertical.

As a result, Enoch came to enjoy the rewards of vertical living. The Bible says he walked with God for *300 years* (and that was *before* Flintstone Vitamins!). The eternal God was his Father and friend, his counselor and companion. He experienced the kind of joy, peace and victory over sin that you crave. In fact, he and God were so "tight," you might say, that one day God gave him a coupon that said, "Go straight to heaven; do not pass through death, do not collect dust in the grave."

The best part of it, though, is that you can be like Enoch. You might not get a nonstop ticket to heaven, but you can live in the vertical . . . if, like Enoch, you pay close attention to the obstacles, steps and rewards of vertical living.

Word Up

Take a few moments to think further about what it means to live "in the vertical" by completing the following:

• Do you face any obstacles to vertical living? What do you think are the three things that most keep you from "walking with God" in holiness and righteousness?

1. anger, my temper, and unwillingness to wait.
2. Meijer
3. Chris

• Take a moment to tell God about each obstacle, and ask Him to show you how to overcome it in the days and weeks ahead, perhaps using Psalm 51:10-12 as a pattern for prayer.

The Obstacles to Vertical Living

7

Liz and the Computer Whiz

*S*andy-haired Liz stared at her computer screen. It was doing things she'd never seen before.

Of course, Richard, whom everyone at school called "Richard the Computer Wizard" sat at the keyboard. Richard knew more about computers than anyone Liz knew, and when he found out that her parents had bought her a Quazar 810 for her birthday almost two months ago, he offered to give her a little free training.

He had spent about five or 10 minutes tinkering with the cables and connections behind the machine before turning it on; now he sat at the keyboard asking Liz a string of questions about how she had used the computer.

"I just basically, like, do my homework and reports on it," she said.

"That's it?" he asked.

She nodded.

"Did you know you could do this?"

Richard tapped a couple keys and a small screen appeared in the upper right corner of the monitor.

"What's that?" Liz asked.

Richard squinted through his wire-rimmed glasses. "Looks like Oprah."

"You mean on TV?"

"Oh, yeah. You can keep one eye on the Shopping Mall Channel while you're doing your homework, and even call in your order through the modem."

"I can?"

"Sure," Richard answered gleefully, tapping more keys. The inset television screen appeared to be changing channels. "What's this?" he asked, apparently to himself. He studied the screen, and finally punched a combination of keys. The television picture suddenly grew to occupy the entire monitor, trading places with the computer screen, which was now in the inset.

"Wow!" Liz said.

"Say you're doing a report," he said, still squinting at the picture on the screen, "and this Education Channel show on Peruvian art comes on TV." He turned and smiled. "A simple command—" he tapped two keys simultaneously— "and the picture is now part of your report." He reversed the two images on the screen again, so that the TV screen returned to the inset. The image of the South American vase that had been on television a moment ago was now on Liz's computer screen . . . in full color.

Liz gasped. "Wow!" she said. "I never knew I could do all that. I've had this computer all this time and never knew these things were even possible!"

Perhaps you've had a similar experience. Some computers have such incredible capabilities, most of us will never understand all the possibilities they possess. It's the same way with the vertical lifestyle. A huge number of Christians honestly don't know it's possible.

They long to be delivered, not only from the *love* of sin, but also from its *power*. They want to believe Paul's words of Romans 8:9 ("You, however, are controlled not by the sinful nature but by the Spirit, if the Spirit of God lives in you"), but their experience sure doesn't match up with Paul's words. They thrill to hear the promise that "we are more than conquerors through him who loved us" (Romans 8:37), but they are resigned to defeat.

This is true of some Christians because *they haven't been told* that the vertical lifestyle is possible. Like Liz, who had never heard that her computer could do such marvelous things, many Christians have never been encouraged to seek anything better than the roller-coaster ride of their earliest experience. Many churches and preachers do not teach that it's possible to break the control of the sinful nature and be controlled instead by the Spirit (Romans 8:9-14).

Many do not know that the vertical lifestyle is possible because *they haven't witnessed it*. Liz's eyes were opened to the possibilities of her Quazar 810 when she *saw* what her machine could do in the hands of Richard the computer wizard. Similarly, many Christians are ignorant of the vertical lifestyle because they haven't seen it—or, if they have, they weren't aware of it. Their eyes are opened to the failures and faults of other Christians, not to the "all-surpassing power" from God (2 Corinthians 4:7) that is displayed in the lives of those who are "walking with God." Those who are living vertically point to Christ, not to themselves, while those who are resigned to defeat point to their own limited experience as evidence that nothing greater is possible.

Finally, a great many don't know that vertical living is possible because *they haven't read the manual*. For two months, Liz had possessed a 600-page computer manual that could have exposed her to all the possibilities of her Quazar; but she never read it, never studied it, never took the time to discover what it said about her new machine.

Similarly, many Christians continue to live in sin and defeat because they don't read the manual, the Bible. They haven't read the clear testimony that "His divine power has given us *everything* we need for life and godliness" (2 Peter 1:3). They haven't read the promise "that we may share in [God's] holiness" (Hebrews 12:10). They haven't read that it is possible "by the Spirit [to] put to death the misdeeds of the body" (Romans 8:13). They haven't read the command to "purify ourselves from everything that contaminates body and spirit, perfecting holiness out of reverence for God" (2 Corinthians 7:1).

Such Christians, if they were somehow to discover the reality of vertical living, might echo Liz's sentiment when she learned what her computer could do. "I've been a Christian all this time," they might say, "and never even knew it was possible to really get off the roller-coaster ride and gain consistent, constant victory over sin. I never realized that the blood of Jesus Christ could cleanse me from *all* sin" (1 John 1:7).

The power of the Spirit of Christ in a Christian's life would put the most sophisticated computer to shame, of course. But all that power is wasted for the person who doesn't know it exists.

Word Up

Have you read the "manual" of vertical living? Take a few moments to apply yourself to the Holy Word of God by completing the following:

- Do you think God would command you to do the impossible? (circle one)

  a. Yes
  b. No
  c. I don't know

- Look up the following commands or biblical standards in your Bible; then check any that you think can be obeyed:

  ✓ 1 Peter 1:14-16   ✓ 1 Thessalonians 4:3-7
  ✓ Colossians 3:5-10   ✓ Ephesians 4:22-24
  ✓ 1 John 3:8-9   ✓ 2 Corinthians 7:1

8

Ward and the Bungee Cord

A bead of sweat trickled down Ward's upper lip, paused a moment, then dropped onto the pavement a hundred feet below.

"How'd I let you talk me into this?" he asked his best friend, Buddy. Ward stood at the edge of a bungee platform, 100 feet in the air, peering down from his breathtaking height at the hard earth at the foot of the tower.

"What?" Buddy countered, as if it were completely unnatural for Ward to fear death or mutilation.

"I can't do this," Ward said. He gripped the railing on either side of him with white knuckles.

"Look, I've checked the cord three times now. You've got nothing to worry about."

"What if this little rubber band snaps?" Ward protested, pointing to the thick, stretchy cord fastened to his left ankle. "You'll have to take me home in a pizza box."

"Will you quit worrying? I told you, I've done this dozens of times. You're not gonna fall; the bungee cord will keep you from falling all the way."

Ward flashed his friend a doubtful look.

"Look," Buddy continued, sweeping his arm around to indicate the small amusement park that stretched below them. "Do you think *Vinny's Fun Farm* would let you jump off a 100-foot tower if it wasn't safe?"

"Well . . ."

"You think your 15 bucks would be worth risking a million-dollar lawsuit? Of course not. And if you don't trust them, trust me; that bungee will stop you long before you hit the ground." He placed a hand on his friend's shoulder. "OK?"

Ward sighed. "I guess you're right," he said.

"They wouldn't have this here if it wasn't safe."

"Exactly! OK, ready? On three . . . one, two, THREE!"

Ward leaped from the tower, protected from harm only by a long, elastic bungee cord. Just as he launched his body into the air, however, a thought occurred to him that seemed strangely important: *Wait a minute! If this isn't dangerous, why did* Vinny's Fun Farm *make me sign a release form before letting me jump?*

Ward's fear seems perfectly natural to many people. In fact, most people would find it pretty difficult to trust their lives to an over-sized rubber band. After all, bungee cords can break; fasteners can fail. Most of us are hesitant to put our faith in such things.

Unfortunately, that kind of thinking—which most of us would say is reasonable in Ward's case—presents an obstacle to vertical living for many people. They may have heard preaching and teaching about Christ's ability to save them from sin; they may know someone who exemplifies the vertical life; they may *even* have "read the manual" and acknowledged the Bible's teaching that the Lord is "able to keep [them] from falling and to present [them] before his glorious presence without fault" (Jude 24), yet they do not or cannot *believe* it.

"You don't understand my family," they may say. "They're impossible! They make it so hard to be a Christian." They cannot believe that the resurrected Christ can actually purify them "from *all* sin" (1 John 1:7).

"I've tried before," they may say, "lots of times. And everything goes pretty well for a while, but before long, I'm giving in to the same old temptations, the same habits, the same sins." They cannot believe that the Savior who conquered sin and death "is able to keep [them] from falling" (Jude 24).

"I could never be holy," they say. "I'm not good enough," or "I'm not smart enough," or "I'm not old enough." They cannot believe that the same Lord who commands His followers to "be holy" (1 Peter 1:16) is strong enough to "enable us to serve him . . . in holiness and righteousness" (Luke 1:74-75).

Are their faults greater than those of Peter, who publicly denied the Lord? He not only obtained forgiveness for his sins, he believed in the risen Lord's power to make men and women holy. He wrote,

> Do not conform to the evil desires you had when you lived in ignorance. But just as he who called you is holy, so be holy in all you do. (1 Peter 1:14-15)

Are their sins deeper than those of David, who committed adultery with Bathsheba and tried to cover up his sin by having her husband killed? He exhibited his belief in God's ability when he cried out, "Create in me a pure heart, O God, and renew a steadfast spirit within me" (Psalm 51:10).

Are their circumstances harder than the apostle Paul, who endured shipwreck, disease, beatings and stoning? He showed his belief in the possibility of victory over the sinful nature when he wrote (from prison!),

> Since, then, you have been raised with Christ, set your hearts on things above. . . . Put to death, therefore, whatever belongs to your earthly nature: sexual immorality, impurity, lust, evil desires and greed. . . . You used to walk in these ways, in the life you once lived. But now you must rid yourselves of all such things . . . since you have taken off your old self with its practices and have put on the new self, which is being renewed in knowledge in the image of its Creator. (Colossians 3:1, 5, 7-10)

Peter, David and Paul lived in the vertical, not because their faults, sins or circumstances were less severe than ours, but because they *believed* God. Instead of trying to make the Word of God conform to their experience, they trusted God to make their experience conform to His Word and its clear commands.

God still rewards that kind of belief.

Word Up

Each of the following verses of Scripture is wrong. See how many statements you can correct by crossing out the wrong part and writing in the correct word or words (check your answers by looking up the verse in your Bible):

1. "[He] is able to keep you from ~~talking in class~~"
   from falling & present you before his
   (Jude 24). *glorious presence w/o fault +*
   w/ great joy.

2. "May God himself, the God of peace, ~~punish~~" *sanctify*

   you through and through" (1 Thessalonians

   5:23).

3. "And so Jesus also suffered outside the city

   gate to make the people ~~mad~~ *holy* through his

   own blood" (Hebrews 13:12).

4. "Make every effort to live in peace with all

   men and to be holy; without holiness no one
   see the Lord
   will ~~please their parents~~" (Hebrews 12:14).

5. "But now that you have been set free from sin

   and have become slaves to God, the benefit you
   holiness, and the result
   reap leads to a ~~better complexion~~" (Romans 6:22).
   is eternal life.

9

The Young and the Restless

$\mathcal{T}$wo women sat in the back pew of a small church. One wore a tight knot of gray hair at the back of her head; the other's silver locks framed her wrinkled face in tightly permed ringlets.

The women waited for the ushers to collect their offering as the church organist played a loud, stirring rendition of *Holy, Holy, Holy*. One of the women fingered a wrinkled dollar bill with white-gloved hands; the other perched her purse on her lap and fished around inside for the right amount.

They attempted to talk to each other over the

strains of the organ, their voices rising with every crescendo of the organist. They leaned closer to each other as the music became louder, until they were exchanging shouts that each other could barely hear.

The music stopped abruptly, just as the woman with the silver perm shouted to the woman with the gray bun, "I soak mine in butter!"

Those two elderly women illustrate what many teenagers and young adults picture when they hear the word "holiness"—perhaps without the comment about butter. Many youth assume the vertical lifestyle is for old women and dying men; they figure it's impractical for someone who's wrestling with things like algebra homework, adolescent humor and active hormones.

But vertical living is *not* just for the old and infirm; in fact, it may be even *more* necessary for the young and the restless!

Think back to what you know about Jesus— the "author and perfecter" of vertical living. According to the Gospel writer Luke, Jesus was living the vertical life, in constant fellowship with His heavenly Father, as a preteen. He was 12 years old when a frantic Joseph and Mary discovered Him in the temple, practicing for His bar mitzvah. When they found Him, they said something like, "Where have You been? We've been worried sick about You! Don't You ever do that again!" Twelve-year-old Jesus didn't respond by saying, "Don't have a cow, man!" He didn't say, "Give Me a break, will ya? All you ever do is yell at Me."

He didn't threaten to run away and get a tattoo. He answered them calmly. "Didn't you know I had to be in My Father's house?" His parents didn't understand what in the world He was talking about (Luke 2:50), but He tried to help them understand that He was simply living a vertical life, a life of constant devotion to His Father—and that was before He entered seventh grade!

Jesus was probably 29 or 30 years old when He began his public ministry; some of the people who followed Him were certainly much younger—perhaps even teenagers!

Only one of Jesus' 12 closest disciples was married (or widowed); the others were apparently young enough to still be looking for brides when Jesus called them, and none had become parents (nor would they, apparently, for a number of years).

The mother of James and John (who are identified in the Gospels as "the sons of Zebedee") once knelt before Jesus and, like a mother asking for her first grader to be given a part in the school play, asked a favor of Jesus. "Grant that one of these two sons of mine may sit at your right and the other at your left in your kingdom" (Matthew 20:21). The mother of these boys was not only still alive, but she was still trying to help her sons get ahead in the world.

That same John, who is called "the disciple Jesus loved" in the Gospel of John, was the last of the Twelve to die. He wrote the Revelation, the last book of the Bible, around 95 A.D., and probably died during the reign of the Roman emperor Trajan, around 98 A.D. We don't know how old John was when he died, but even if he were almost 90 years old then, *he would have been a teenager when he joined the band of Jesus' disciples.*

John was probably not the only youthful member of Jesus' band of Twelve. Jesus not only tried to teach His disciples about vertical living; He led them in a youthful lifestyle as well. They hiked up and down the length of Galilee and Judea; they traveled light and ate on the run; they slept under trees and in barns or crashed at friends' houses, sleeping on the floor. Jesus and His followers joked and argued and talked about the future; their words and actions were full of life and vigor and whimsy; they challenged traditions and offended the establishment.

The Gospels are largely an account of *young* men and women learning about the vertical life; they abound with accounts of the young and the restless learning from Jesus, who was referred to in the original words of the Isaac Watts hymn as "the *young* Prince of Glory."

In fact, living in the vertical may be *more* necessary for the young. Older people don't need to worry about puberty and its effects; they're

not faced with figuring out male-female rela-
tionships for the first time in their lives. Old
men and women needn't concern themselves
with balancing teachers' demands and parents'
expectations; they don't have to contend with
geometry, chemistry and drivers' ed. at the
same time. Adults don't have to cope with rag-
ing hormones that drive your interest in the
opposite sex (and at the same time destroy
your complexion with acne).

Vertical living does not make all that stuff
easy; it is, however, the only means to victory
in such things. A lifestyle of constant dependence upon and fellowship with God is the
only way for a teenager or young adult to
please God—and squeeze the most youthful
enjoyment out of life.

Word Up

Many of us picture the participants in the
Gospels as gray-bearded men and matronly
women. See if the following support that image.

- Read John 20:1-9, John's account of the resurrection. The passage doesn't mention the participants' ages. What age do you think Mary,
Peter and John were at the time of these
events? What physical activity do they perform? They were probably no older then 30.
They run to the tumb

- Read John 21:15-19. Notice Jesus' choice of words: He talks about when Peter was "youn*ger*," and a future time when Peter will be "old." What do those words imply about Peter at the time of that conversation? In Jesus' estimation, was Peter: (circle one)

  a. younger
  b. young
  c. middle-aged
  d. old

- Have you ever thought of the vertical life as something reserved for older people? Why or why not?

  No, because we all need to live good christian lives, I just don't think many young people do it.

10

Optional Equipment

*Y*ou haven't been this excited in a long time. You don't even finish your McDonald's French fries, because you're impatient to finish lunch and get to where you're going. Fi-

63

nally, after what seems painfully close to a ba-zillion years, your dad swallows the last bite of his Big Mac. You jump up from the table.

"Let's go," you announce impatiently. You're going with your mom and dad to buy a new family car. OK, so it's not going to be *your* car, but you're still excited. You can't wait till your friends see you riding around town in a new sports car or four-wheel-drive vehicle.

You arrive at the dealership with your parents. Your mom and dad saunter into the showroom, while you immediately head for a cherry-red sports car sitting right inside the door.

"Look at this one, Dad!" you call excitedly. "It's got a leather interior and a CD player with 12-inch speakers!"

Your father nods and begins looking at a dorky-looking car in the corner. Standing next to a black four-wheel-drive utility vehicle you try the mature, logical approach: "Hey, Dad! We'd never get stuck in the snow in this like we did at Aunt Esmerelda's house last Christmas!"

Your father appears to be talking to the sales-man about the box-like model he's standing be-side. Your mom is sitting in the passenger seat. You walk over to your mom and stick your head in the window.

"He's not thinking about getting *this* one, is he?" you ask your mom, adding a silent prayer along the lines of, "Please God, no, no, don't let him buy this one."

"I think so, sweetheart," she says. "It *is* in our price range."

"No!" you cry. "Mom, don't let him buy this one."

"Why not?" she asks.

"Why not?" you echo. "There's hardly room for anybody in there."

"I'm quite comfortable."

"And it's just so . . . so plain."

"It has a radio," she says, pointing to a device the size of a postage stamp. "AM *and* FM."

"A radio?" you shout. "Not even a tape deck? No CD player? No 12-inch speakers? No equalizer? No bass booster?"

"That's all optional, sweetheart. We don't need all that stuff. Besides, you know your father likes to listen to talk radio."

You stare at your mother. *Optional?* How can she say such things? Is she purposely trying to destroy your life? You stare at this woman, this alien being who thinks that a decent stereo system is *optional* equipment. You expect her at any moment to sprout a second head or peel off the rubbery cover of her android face . . . but she does neither. She simply stares back innocently, smiling sweetly.

Perhaps you've never had quite that experience. But you know, nonetheless, that every new car is equipped with a set of features that is called "standard equipment"; that is, those features pretty much come with every car and are included in the price of the car itself. Then, of course, there are "extras," or "options," for which you usually pay extra. Such things as CD players, leather interiors, sunroofs and fog lights are usually considered optional equipment.

The problem is, some people classify the vertical lifestyle as "optional equipment." One of the greatest barriers preventing many people from experiencing victory over sin is the belief that such an experience is "optional." It's like a sunroof; it's nice to have, they figure, but one can very easily get along without it.

But that's dead wrong. The Word of God makes it painfully clear—so clear, in fact, that many people reason that the Bible must not mean what it says. The writer of Hebrews wrote, "Make every effort to live in peace with all men and to be holy; without holiness no one will see the Lord" (Hebrews 12:14).

That's pretty blunt, isn't it? If you want to see Amy Grant in concert, you need to obtain a ticket. If you want a football scholarship from a major university, you need to sign a letter of intent. Likewise, says the writer of Hebrews, if you want to see the Lord, the ticket is holiness. If you remember chapter two, you remember that sinful men and women cannot approach a holy God.

Now, remember, those words were written to Christians—first century Jewish Christians, in all likelihood. And he's informing them, point blank, that holiness is not an option . . . it is standard equipment for the Christian life.

The apostle John put it another way:

> Dear friends, now we are children of God, and what we will be has not yet been made known. But we know that when he appears, we shall be like him, for we shall see him as he is. Everyone who has this hope in him purifies himself, just as he is pure.
>
> Everyone who sins breaks the law; in fact, sin is lawlessness. But you know that he appeared so that he might take away our sins. And in him is no sin. No one who lives in him keeps on sinning. No one who continues to sin has either seen him or known him. (1 John 3:2-6)

That's why living in the vertical is so important. That's why it's standard—not optional—equipment. Because it is the only way to obey God's clear command: "Be holy, because I am holy" (Leviticus 11:44, 45; 19:2; 20:7).

Word Up

Examine the biblical requirement of Christian holiness by reading the following statements and then indicating whether you think each is true or false:

1. It is God's will that you should be sanctified.
 T F

2. God reserves the blessing of holiness for special people.

    T   (F)

3. God doesn't really expect us to stop sinning.

    (T) F

4. Without holiness no one will see God.

    (T) F

5. If anyone does not have the Spirit of Christ, he does not belong to Christ.

    (T) F

6. You have been set free from sin.

    (T) F

11

Indiana Jones and the Temple of Gloom

*T*he great explorer and adventurer sat on the crumbling steps of the 12th-century Hindu temple. His elbows were propped on his knees and his chin rested in his hands.

"C'mon, Indy," said his sidekick, Shorty. "Let's *do* something."

"What do you want to do, kid?" Jones stared into the jungle, not even looking at the boy.

"We could steal a ninth-century Khmer artifact and escape the country by crawling on our bellies through rice paddies," the boy suggested.

"Done that," the explorer answered.

"OK, then," the boy offered. "We could swim through eel-infested waters in Hong Kong to attach a bomb to the hull of a junk, leaving ourselves just enough time to wrestle a giant squid and swim away without getting blown up ourselves."

Indy sighed. "Been there."

"Well, we could always parachute into the mouth of an active volcano while crazed Ninja assassins pursue us on hang gliders."

The adventurer rolled his eyes. "Did that last week . . . with a time bomb strapped to my chest."

This time it was Shorty's turn to sigh. "I give up, then. *You* think of something."

Indiana Jones stared, unmoving, into the jungle that surrounded him and his partner. A fly buzzed around his head and landed on his ear; he didn't even shake it off. Finally, he exhaled loudly and turned to Shorty.

"I suppose we could both commit ourselves completely to God and pursue a life of holiness."

Shorty's head rotated slowly until his full face was turned toward the great explorer and archaeologist. Indy stared back at him, straight-faced. Finally, as if someone had flipped a switch controlling them both, they simultaneously erupted into uncontrollable laughter.

"Hoo! That's a good one, Indy!"

"You thought I was serious there for a minute, didn't you?"

"Get serious," the boy answered, fighting to catch a breath amid his laughter. "Holiness!"

"Wouldn't *that* be exciting!" Indy cackled, slapping a knee and rolling down the stone steps of the ancient temple.

Go ahead and laugh, Indy and Shorty. Your idea of holiness isn't much different from that of most people—including many Christians. A lot of people have the opinion that a life of wholehearted, single-minded devotion to God is *bo-ring!* They figure that, in terms of excitement, the vertical life ranks right up there with school lunches, watching PBS and helping Aunt Helen clip her toenails. They think that sanctification saps all the fun out of life. "Holiness would be OK," they might reason, "if it wasn't so *boring*. I mean, it might be all right for monks and ministers; but I like a little excitement in my life, you know?"

If that's the case with you, then the vertical life is exactly what you need. The vertical life will plunge you into exploits and adventures you could never have imagined. Living in constant fellowship with God will breed a new excitement in your life, a new fulfillment and satisfaction that you could never achieve without the Spirit of God. Holy living will open your eyes to opportunities, challenges and possibilities that you never knew existed.

Moses had been living a pretty ordinary life as a shepherd in the desert of Midian when he responded to God's call and began living in intimate, daily fellowship with God. From that point on, he became a world traveler, a political leader, a miracle worker, a songwriter, a judge, a mountain climber and a high-stakes negotiator. He was even called back to earth centuries after his death for a top-secret conference with Jesus Himself! Not too boring, is it?

Daniel was probably your typical rich kid when his country was conquered and he was taken prisoner to Babylon. But he was also living in the vertical. As a result, he became an innovative nutritionist, a big shot in a big government, a convict, an authority on dreams, a handwriting expert, a lion tamer, a prophet and a best-selling author. The vertical life sure didn't put him into a coma.

The apostle Paul went from a plotter against the church to a planter of churches, and the results of a vertical lifestyle for Paul included stints as an escape artist, tentmaker, missionary, political prisoner, lawyer, rabble rouser, snake charmer, shipwreck survivor and foreign correspondent. Of course, Paul never went bungee jumping or skydiving; he didn't need to. Living in the vertical made his life about as exciting as he could stand.

The Spirit of God can take you places no map will ever show. He may stir you to do things Indiana Jones could never attempt. He might change your life in ways that would make you say "No way!" if he were to reveal His plan to you right now. He will definitely test you and challenge you and stretch you and make you shake your head in wonder at what He has done with you and through you.

The vertical life will not necessarily get you thrown into prison or enable you to part water like you would cut a cake; but it's not boring, that's for sure. In fact, the danger is just the opposite; a life lived in fellowship with the God who originated space travel, invented laser technology before humans discovered fire, and developed the most sophisticated CPU in the world (the human brain), might just be more excitement than you can handle.

Word Up

Take a few moments to think about the exciting challenge of the vertical life by completing the following:

- Read Hebrews 11:32-12:1. Which of the challenges or achievements in verses 33-38 sound boring to you?

    None of this sounds exciting, actually. It sounds kind of painful.

- According to Hebrews 12:1, the example and testimony of the heroes of the faith mentioned in chapter 11 should cause you to (check all that apply):

__throw caution to the wind
__throw away your whole CD collection
  (except for Amy Grant)
√ throw off everything that hinders
__give up on the vertical life
√ throw off the sin that so easily entangles
__join a monastery or convent
√ run with perseverance the race marked
  out for you
__throw your geometry book down the
  nearest manhole

- Spend a few moments in prayer, basing your
  prayer on Hebrews 12:1. (For example, you
  might say, "Lord, since You did such incredible things for people like Abraham and
  Gideon and all those others in the Bible, help
  me to throw off everything that hinders me,
  especially . . ." etc.)

12

True Grit

$\mathcal{T}$he cowboy never saw the snake. He had been gathering wood for his small campfire, preparing to heat some coffee and beans for a lonely supper after a hard day of riding, when he heard a brief rattle and felt a sharp pain in his right hand. He pulled his hand back and looked at it in the moonlight. It had already begun to swell.

He was alone in the San Juan Mountains of southern Colorado; there was nowhere to ride, and no one to call for help. He looked around him at the sky, seemingly empty of stars, and the harsh, unforgiving terrain that surrounded him.

"Not where I planned to die," he muttered. He reached his left hand behind his body and withdrew the knife that hung from his belt over his right hip. He grimaced at the burning pain in his hand and squinted at his horse. "So we'll just have to see about that."

Working clumsily with his left hand, he dug the tip of the knife into the flesh of his right hand, cutting away the skin around the snake-bite. After a few moments of hurried work, he threw the knife down onto the ground. Gripping his right hand in his left, he raised the bloody back of his hand to his mouth and repeatedly sucked the blood and poison into his mouth and spit it out in the dirt.

After many moments of such work, the sweating cowhand ripped his kerchief from around his neck and wrapped it around the throbbing hand. He stumbled to the pile of wood he had started to build for a fire, lit it and leaned against the saddle he had earlier removed from his horse. It might be a day or two, he reasoned, but he was hopeful that he had extracted enough of the poison to save his own life. Suddenly, his eyes rolled back into his head, and he lost consciousness.

Now, *that* is "true grit." That cowboy probably didn't enjoy digging around in his own flesh with a knife, nor sucking the poison out of his hand as he did, but he gritted his teeth and did what had to be done. He displayed gutsy, unflinching determination, sort of like Rambo, the Sylvester Stallone creation whose grit became a pattern for movie tough guys, from Jean-Claude Van Damme to Steven Seagal.

Believe it or not, a lot of people think it takes that kind of grit to live in the vertical. They imagine that "holy" living requires a "grit-your-teeth" struggle against sin, the flesh and the devil, a struggle in which only the strong survive. They figure that the way to holiness is a way of blood, sweat and tears.

"I need to try harder," they tell themselves, "and *then* I can really be a good Christian."

"If I do this," they may decide, "and *don't* do that, then I'll be holy."

"Oh Lord," they may even pray, "I'm gonna change, I really am. If it takes every ounce of strength I have, I'm gonna resist temptation from now on."

But such thinking (and praying) is actually an *obstacle* to vertical living. It fosters a mistaken idea of the vertical lifestyle, one that opens the door, not to victory, but to more and more defeat.

Vertical living doesn't require a "grit-your-teeth" struggle. Your hope of living a holy and godly life (2 Peter 3:11) will never be realized as a result of "true grit." No amount of effort will make you holy.

Holiness cannot be achieved; it can only be bestowed. You can't experience victory over sin by *trying*; you can only do it by *trusting*.

God made that clear way back in the days of Ezekiel the prophet, when he promised,

> I will give you a new heart and put a new spirit within you; and I will remove the heart of stone from your flesh and give you a heart of flesh. And I will put My Spirit within you and *cause* you to walk in My statutes, and you will be careful to observe My ordinances (Ezekiel 36:26-27, NASB; emphasis added).

You see, it's not your job to try to live in the vertical; it is your job to trust the Spirit of God to *cause* you to live in the vertical. Your part is trusting, not trying.

Imagine James Bond, the famous 007, being called in to the headquarters of M1, the British intelligence agency. His boss rises from his chair and comes around to the front of the desk to meet Bond.

"James," he says, "I wanted to show you the latest device our laboratories have developed."

"Fine," replies the secret agent. "I'd like to see it."

"Well," Bond's boss answers. "I'm afraid you can't. You see, Bond, it's invisible."

"Oh. What does it do?"

"A lot of things, Bond! It goes wherever you go. It doesn't freeze when it's cold, it doesn't melt when it's hot. It can steer you in the right direction. It can give you auxiliary power to tackle feats which would otherwise be impossible. And it will keep your heart pure and your conduct holy."

Bond clears his throat. "I see," he says awkwardly. "How do I activate the device?"

"Oh, it's already activated. You simply submit to its control, and let it handle every circumstance you face . . . it will do the rest."

That's sort of what living in the vertical is like, only instead of a super-secret device, you have the Spirit of Christ living inside you. His Spirit is able to *cause you* to walk with God; His power can *make you* careful to obey His commandments. That doesn't mean you have to do nothing (in fact, the steps you must take will be covered in chapters 18-25). It simply means God—and God alone—has the ability to make you holy.

Word Up

You can further explore God's ability to save you from sin and "sanctify you through and through" by completing the following:

- Read Romans 7:18-25. Paul says that a Christian can experience deliverance from sin (check all that apply):

  √ through repeated and determined effort
  __ through church membership
  __ through listening to Christian radio
  √ through Jesus Christ our Lord
  __ through diet and exercise

- Look up the word "trust" in a dictionary. Which of the definitions given do you think the author means when he says, "You can't experience victory over sin by *trying;* you can only do it by *trusting?*" Write that definition below.

trust: When you turn everything over to someone else, and they take care of you.

God wants you to trust in him to get everything done. If you try to hard, God won't allow you to do anything.

13

Barking Up the Wrong Tree

That dog won't hunt!"
Elmer slammed the cabin door behind him
and tossed his hunting rifle into the corner.

"What's the matter this time, Elmer?" Elmer's mother stirred a wooden spoon around and around in a big metal pot the size of some foreign cars. Elmer closed his mouth and sniffed in the smell created by the pot full of soup beans and ham scraps.

"Why, that ain't no bird dog," he said. Elmer had traded a worthless old baseball glove that had been signed by some girl called "Babe Ruth" for an eight-year-old bird dog that used to be called "Prince." The man he'd traded with said the dog had a different name now, but Elmer couldn't pronounce it, so he just went ahead and called him Prince.

"Sit down and have some beans," his mother said. "You'll feel better after your belly's full."

"No, it's no good, Maw. That dog I traded for is plumb worthless as a bird dog. He goes off chasing after everything on legs. He's always barkin' up a tree after some squirrel he's run after when he should be flushing out some birds for me to shoot."

"Well," his mother said, "that's all right, son. I don't like eatin' no bird meat anyway. I think the feathers kinda ruin the taste."

Elmer's dog isn't the only one barking up the wrong tree. Many people miss out on the vertical lifestyle because they make a similar mistake. They trip over one of the most common obstacles to biblical holiness in seeking an "experience" instead of Christ, desiring "holiness" instead of the Holy One.

It is natural to want a special blessing from God. It is understandable for a person to desire the benefits of a clean heart. But holiness will not be found by those who are seeking an emotional "joy ride"; it will not be experienced by those who seek to elevate themselves to a new level of righteousness.

It is a paradox, a thing that seems to contradict itself, but God bestows holiness on those who hunger and thirst after righteousness, not because they desire a blessing, but because they desire Christ Himself. It will be found only by those who:

Seek to know Christ. Paul the apostle wrote to the Philippian church that his desire was to "gain Christ and be found in him, not having a righteousness of my own that comes from the law, but that which is through faith in Christ—the righteousness that comes from God and is by faith. I want to know Christ and the power of his resurrection and the fellowship of sharing in his sufferings" (Philippians 3:8b-10). Paul was not primarily seeking some sublime experience; he sought Christ, to know Him and be found in Him . . . and even to share in His sufferings.

Seek to glorify Christ. Earlier in that third chapter of Philippians, Paul said "we . . . glory in Christ Jesus, and . . . put no confidence in the flesh" (Philippians 3:3). Paul's goal was not to be identified and pointed out as someone who was holy; it was to glorify Jesus as the Holy One.

Seek to boast in Christ. Some who have testified to the experience of holiness have invited doubt or disrepute because their testimony has focused on *their* holiness, as if it were their accomplishment, not Christ's. But Paul told the church at Corinth, "Christ Jesus . . . has become for us wisdom from God—that is, our righteousness, holiness and redemption. Therefore, as it is written, 'Let him who boasts boast in the Lord' " (1 Corinthians 1:30-31).

The Christian who sincerely wants to know Christ (instead of a euphoric experience), glorify Him (instead of himself or herself) and boast in Him (instead of in his or her accomplishment) is truly hungry for righteousness, "the righteousness that comes from God and is by faith" (Philippians 3:9).

All the others are barking up the wrong tree.

Word Up

Paul's letter to the Philippians contains a stirring account of his desires and motivations.

- Read Philippians 3:7-11. As you read, note on the chart below the things Paul considered unimportant and those things he desired:

	unimportant	*important*
v. 7	Whatever was to his profit.	Taking a loss for christ
v. 8	Everything he has lost in the past.	The surpassing greatness of knowing Christ

	unimportant	*important*
v. 9	Righteousness from the law.	The righteousness from Christ.
v. 10		Knowing Christ + gaining power through resurection
v. 11		Attaining resurection from dead.

- Read Philippians 3:12. Do you find encouragement in this verse? What do you think it means? What do you think Paul means by "that for which Christ Jesus took hold of me?" (See if First Thessalonians 3:13 provides a clue.) – yes, because Paul is still working and learning from God even though he is saved.

  – Paul wants us to continue to work after God's taken over our lives.

  – Paul means that Christ took ahold of his foot and directed his steps.

14

Eight Expectations

*B*y now you're probably getting the idea that there are more than a few obstacles to the vertical life. If that's what you're thinking, you're right.

Why wouldn't it be so? The Bible says that "The reason the Son of God appeared was to destroy the devil's work" (1 John 3:8). If you were the devil, and you knew that the Son of God was capable of completely destroying your power over men and women, what would you do? Wouldn't you create as many obstacles as possible to keep people from understanding and believing that they no longer have to be slaves to sin (Romans 6:18)?

And that's exactly what the adversary has done; that's why there are so many obstacles to vertical living—not because it is hard for us, but because it is disastrous for the enemy! And one of the key strategies of the devil is to create false expectations of what it means to live in the vertical, faulty images of what a holy Christian life should be, and with those false ideas to prevent a young man or woman from discovering the way of holiness (Isaiah 35:8). What are some of those wrong ideas? Let's look at eight expectations that often present an obstacle to vertical living:

1. *The first of these faulty expectations is the idea that a holy life brings constant joy and serenity.* The young man or woman who is living in the vertical *will* experience the full measure of joy that Jesus promised (John 17:13) and the perfect peace that comes only from a vertical lifestyle (Isaiah 26:3). But even Jesus cried (John 11:35). The sinless Lord of glory was "a man of sorrows, and familiar with suffering" (Isaiah 53:3). The vertical lifestyle doesn't insulate a person from disappointment, bereavement or pain, though it does equip him or her with a greater ability to endure such things.

2. *Another faulty expectation is that the vertical lifestyle brings freedom from temptation.* Some people honestly expect that, once they begin to "serve [God] without fear in holiness and righteousness" (Luke 1:74-75), they will no longer meet with temptation. They imagine that they will be able to skate through life, never battling temptation again. They forget that Jesus Him-

self was tempted, not just once, and not just in a few areas, but "in every way, just as we are" (Hebrews 4:15). The Christian who is living in the vertical will be delivered from sin—but he or she will not be exempted from temptation.

3. *Another false expectation of the holy life is that it involves relief from natural consequences.* Living in the vertical won't correct the bad haircut you got last week; it won't prevent tooth decay caused by eating too many Sweet Tarts. Or, to choose a far more serious example, an alcoholic who commences the vertical life will experience cleansing from sin and power to overcome his addiction; but if his liver has been damaged because of his drinking, he will still have to bear the natural consequences of his actions.

4. *A faulty impression many people have of the life of holiness is that it will bring deliverance from human frailty or imperfections.* A life of holiness is not a life free from mistakes or maladies. For example, you may still (however innocently) "say the wrong thing" at a party and get a friend mad at you. You will still mispronounce people's names and forget to relay phone messages; you may still get runny noses and (unfair as it may seem) a big, hairy zit the night before the junior prom. Those things are all part of being a human. The vertical life doesn't guarantee no more bad hair days.

5. *A common expectation is that the vertical lifestyle is no more than spiritual maturity.* Spiritual maturity should be the goal of every Christian. Paul

wrote of his desire that "the body of Christ may be built up until we all reach unity in the faith and in the knowledge of the Son of God and become mature, attaining to the whole measure of the fullness of Christ" (Ephesians 4:12-13). He spoke of spiritual maturity as something that will come, in time. But practically in the next breath he said, "Put off your old self . . . and . . . put on the new self, created to be like God in true righteousness and holiness" (4:22-24). A child that has been playing in mud puddles all day will one day grow up, that's for sure; but he doesn't have to wait until then to wash up. He can be clean now. That's holiness.

6. *Another faulty expectation is that holiness is a "reformation."* Some people imagine that Christ makes us holy by taking our lives, applying a touch here, a bit of spackle and a dab of paint there and repairs what was wrong with us. But holiness is not a repair job; it's a demolition job! Christ wants to blow up the building of our lives and erect a whole new structure, one that uses the best materials and produces the greatest results. He wants to build from the ground up. He's not interested in reformation; He wants to ignite a revolution in us.

7. *Still another false expectation of the life of holiness is that it is simply a suppression of the sin nature.* Picture a jack-in-the-box, the kind you used to play with as a child. Every time that puppet clown popped out of the box, what did you do? You stuffed him back in, right? Many

people imagine holiness to be like that. They figure that it just means stuffing their stubborn sinful nature "back in the box" every time it pops out. But that's not how it works. Instead, imagine that you received a new toy that made that jack-in-the-box seem so unappealing that you just stopped winding the crank. You were so enamored with your new toy that the jack-in-the-box didn't just get pushed aside . . . it disappeared from your mind. That's an imperfect illustration, but it's more like what happens when the Spirit of Christ sanctifies you; the fullness of Christ fills you . . . and it just seems like there's no room for anything else.

8. *Finally, a false expectation many people have of the holy life is that it is a life of sinless perfection.* Some people imagine that holiness makes it impossible for a person to sin. Samuel Logan Brengle, a famous preacher of holiness, wrote,

It is an unscriptural and dangerous doctrine that there is any state of grace in this world from which we cannot fall. . . . While here, we are in the enemy's country, and must watch and pray and daily examine ourselves, and keep ourselves in the love of God, lest we fall from His grace and make shipwreck our faith. But while we may fall, thank God holiness is a state from which we need not fall . . .*

*(From *Heart Talks on Holiness*, Salvationist Publishing and Supplies, London, 1897. p.10)

As the apostle John wrote, "My dear children, I write this to you so that you *will not sin*" (1 John 2:1). In other words, John considered it perfectly possible for a Christian not to sin; but in that same verse, he acknowledges that sin is always possible for a Christian: "But if anybody does sin, we have one who speaks to the Father in our defense—Jesus Christ, the Righteous One."

These eight expectations are not the only false ideas people have about the vertical lifestyle; they are, perhaps, the most common and the most destructive. Such ideas prevent many from experiencing, and many more from seeking, a life of constant fellowship with God and consistent victory over sin. But in spite of such obstacles, there are still those who "are controlled not by the sinful nature but by the Spirit" (Romans 8:9).

Word Up

Explore your expectations of the vertical lifestyle by completing the following:

- Have you entertained any of the above expectations? If so, which one(s)?

  Yes, the jack in the box theory and the reformation theory.

• Are there any of the above that you still believe? If so, which one(s)?

No

• Read First John 1:9 and 2:1. How do you think these verses apply to you? Consider using these verses as a pattern for personal prayer today. (For example, "Father, I confess my sins, especially _____. I thank You that You are faithful and just to forgive my sins. I ask Your forgiveness, and ask You also to cleanse me from all unrighteousness right now," etc.)

They tell me that Jesus will forgive my sins, all of them. And purify my heart.

15

Great Expectations (NOT!)

*Y*ou arrive home from school the Friday before your 16th birthday and enter the front
door to the sound of 20 friends and relatives
shouting, "Surprise!"

The living room is decorated with streamers
and balloons. You wonder how your best
friend got there ahead of you. Your mom starts
smothering you with embarrassing attention.
Your aunt and uncle are there, and you notice
that your six-year-old cousin has already been
sampling the birthday cake: chocolate frosting
rings his mouth. The chattering of other friends
and relatives fill your ears, and you let your

book bag slide to the floor as you notice the embarrassingly cute "Sweet 16" banner strung across the room.

Your mom ushers you into the "birthday seat," a kitchen chair wrapped in a sheet and decorated to look like a throne; you wonder if other kids have to endure this kind of humiliation on their 16th birthdays. You flash a look at your best friend that's designed to say, "Tell anyone at school about this, and I'll inflict bodily harm on you."

"Please, Mom, don't embarrass me," you whisper, but she pats your head and announces that everyone in the room is going to take turns relating their funniest childhood memory of you. As your Aunt Zelda starts to tell the story of the time you lost your swimsuit in the ocean, you silently pray that God would do for you what He did for Daniel and miraculously shut Aunt Zelda's mouth.

Finally, after what seems an eternity, "story time" ends, and your mom announces that it's gift-giving time. You glance around and notice that there are no gift-wrapped packages in the room. You flash a questioning look at your mom.

"You'll have to *find* your gifts," she says, and you sigh, as if she'd just told you you have to eat all the vegetables on your plate. "I suggest you start out in the garage."

OK, you think. *Just go along with this. It'll soon be over.* You march to the garage and begin rummaging around among the boxes and tools. Suddenly, you turn and face the car . . . there's a gift-wrapped package on the front seat of the new car that sits beside your mom's minivan.

You open the driver's side door and grip the package, looking around on the floor for any others. It's the only one.

You rip open the wrapping to find a new sweater. You turn and smile broadly at your mom and the other guests who stand just inside the door, watching.

"Thanks," you mumble.

"Do you really like it?" your mom asks.

You nod.

"It's not too small?"

You glance at the tag inside the sweater's collar. "No, it's great, Mom, really."

She walks over to you and extends her hand. "Here's the keys," she says, and drops a set of car keys into your open hand.

You blink. Suddenly, a shiver of excitement rides down your spine like a group of screaming teenagers on the first slope of a roller-coaster ride. *They're giving me the car!*

You scream. You jump out of the car and run around it, then dive back behind the steering wheel. *They're giving me the car!*

Of course, that's ridiculous. You would have known as soon as you saw that new car in the garage that it was your 16th birthday present. You're probably right. But, believe it or not, there are many people who make a similar mistake regarding the vertical life; they expect something too small.

Biblical holiness is a great work of God. It is the destruction of the devil's work (1 John 3:8). It is participation in the very nature of God (2 Peter 1:4). It is an escape from the corruption in the world caused by evil desires (2 Peter 1:4). It is the death of the "old you," and the resurrection of a "new you" in the image of Jesus Christ.

But some people misunderstand; they expect far too little, and so they miss the fullness of the Christ life. They may experience victory in one area, and think that means they're living the vertical life. They may finally, after repeated efforts, quit smoking or drinking or cussing, and so think that they have experienced holiness, while inside they are still resentful, impatient, unkind, jealous or proud. They may discover a new joy in sharing the gospel with others and mistake that for a holy life, while they still live according to their sinful natures in other areas. They may develop new skills in Bible study and mistake those skills for the "righteousness that comes by faith" (Hebrews 11:7), while they are still slaves to sin.

The vertical life is not simply shedding outward habits or developing new skills; it is far more radical, far more fundamental, far more pivotal than that. It does not involve conformity to certain beliefs or behaviors; it involves *transformation*. It is not accomplished by improving your mind; it comes about through the *renewing* of your mind. It does not just mean giving up certain outward things; it is a revolution that Christ accomplishes in you *from the inside out!* It is the fulfillment of the apostle Paul's charge:

> I urge you, brothers, in view of God's mercy, to offer your bodies as living sacrifices, holy and pleasing to God—this is your spiritual act of worship. Do not conform any longer to the pattern of this world, but be transformed by the renewing of your mind. (Romans 12:1-2)

Such a radical transformation can only be accomplished, of course, by the Spirit of Christ in you . . . and He is not only able to help you break bad habits and develop new skills, He is "able to do immeasurably more than all we ask or imagine, according to his power that is at work within us" (Ephesians 3:20). That includes the ability to "put off your old self . . . to be made new in the attitude of your minds; and to put on the new self, created to be like God in true righteousness and holiness" (4:22-24).

Word Up

Do you expect too little from your walk with God? Take a few moments to answer that question by completing the following:

• Read Ephesians 3:14-21.

- Now look at verses 20-21. According to these verses, *who* is able?

  What is He able to do?

  more then all we ask or imagine

  What do you think that includes?

  Things we need & we don't know what we do.

  Where is His power at work?

  with in us.

  In light of what verses 20-21 say, do you think He can make you "holy and pleasing to God?"

- Read through Ephesians 3:1-21 again, only this time as a prayer, substituting "me" and "my" for "you," "your," "we" and "us."

16

The Raccoon Trap

*R*icky Raccoon slammed the door of his tree and stalked off into the woods that surrounded his home.

"She can be such a pain sometimes," he said. His mom had refused to excuse him from the dinner table until he'd eaten every last crayfish on his plate. "She treats me like a little baby."

Ricky was almost a year old and, as he constantly reminded his mother, in human years he would be a teenager. But she continued to call him her "little Ricky," although he was already much larger than his two older sisters.

"Ricky," his mother called from behind him. "Don't stay out too late. Make sure you're home by sunrise."

Ricky didn't answer; he silently resolved to

come home only when he felt like it.

Suddenly, about 500 feet from his front door, the moon's reflection off a shiny object caught his eye. He froze and peered into the tiny clearing beside the stream he liked to visit. (He'd once brought Rachel Raccoon, the prettiest raccoon he'd ever seen, to that very spot and tried to kiss her, but she had pulled a fish out of the stream and slapped the side of his head with it.)

Ricky investigated and discovered that the shiny object was a pretty silver necklace of some kind in a wire box with a large hole in the top. He looked around. He tried to pick up the box to shake the sparkling necklace out, but the box was too heavy.

Suddenly, determined to have the shiny object, he thrust his paw through the hole and gripped the necklace. It was his! He pulled his arm back to withdraw the necklace from the box, but his paw was stuck. He had been able to put his paw in, but he couldn't get it out— because it was now balled into a fist, wrapped around the string of shining silver. He tried repeatedly to yank his fist out of the trap, but he couldn't get it out while still holding on to the necklace.

Ricky's mournful cries of frustration and fear attracted the attention of the trap's owner, a young boy who lived nearby, who took Ricky home, dressed him in funny clothes and treated him like a puppy.

Sad, isn't it? Poor Ricky. If only he had figured out that holding on to that silly necklace was the only thing that trapped him; if he had just let go of it, he could have been free.

Ricky's fate is a lot like many young men and women who want to live vertically, walking with God and enjoying victory over sin, but are trapped because they insist on holding on to their pride. You might say that "pride is their necklace" (Psalm 73:6); they don't realize that if they could just let go of self, they could be free.

Some think that the vertical life is for children and old women, and they don't want to be mistaken for either. So, like a raccoon gripping a shiny necklace in a crude trap, they unwittingly choose bondage over freedom.

Others figure that they've got too much going for them (good looks, maybe, or popularity, or something else) to live a life of righteousness and holiness before God just yet. So they stubbornly hold on to the very pride that denies them fulfillment and satisfaction beyond their wildest dreams.

Still others think that it's more impressive to debate the Bible than to live it, so they puff their chests out and condescendingly inform others that holiness teaching is simplistic and unscholarly, not realizing if they would just let go of their pride, they could not only see the Bible's clear command to "be holy"—they could, through the Spirit of Christ, obey it.

By contrast, the individual who is able to recognize that "[God] mocks proud mockers, but gives grace to the humble" (Proverbs 3:34) and let go of his or her pride, will receive far more in return. It's like exchanging an old, beat-up hubcap for a brand new customized cherry-red sports car with a sunroof; you suddenly become aware of how little you liked that hubcap in the first place!

Word Up

Take a few moments to consider any obstacle to the vertical life you face by completing the following:

- Read Hebrews 12:1. This verse speaks of sin as a "snare" (see especially NKJV); is pride a snare for you? If so, describe how it keeps you from experiencing the vertical life:

  Sometimes but not often

  If not, what sin or sins are most likely to "ensnare" you?

  Chris, sexual pleasure

- Use Psalm 131 as a pattern for prayer as you search your heart for any pride that keeps you from experiencing deliverance from sin.

17

Great Balls of Fire!

The Disney film *The Rocketeer* includes a scene in which Cliff, a test pilot, and Peavy, his mentor, discover an experimental jet pack that had been hidden in their hangar by an international spy ring.

Cliff and Peavy fashion a futuristic safety helmet and run a few tests, but they resist the temptation to use the dangerous device—until, in the midst of an air show, a pilot begins to lose control of his plane. Cliff thinks immediately of the rocket pack. He dashes into the hangar, straps the powerful rocket pack on his back, dons the helmet and flips a switch.

With a mighty burst of flame, he blasts into the air, straight up. He performs a few acrobatic flips in the air, then sweeps past the crowded spectator stands, his arms spread like wings. He shoots into the air toward the crippled plane; his head crashes through the floorboards at the pilot's feet. The pilot panics, yanks the throttle and knocks himself unconscious.

Cliff switches the power pack off and climbs to the open cockpit of the biplane. His efforts to rouse the pilot are unsuccessful, so he pulls up on the throttle and throws himself from the plane. He begins free-falling toward the ground, until he finds the power switch and the rocket on his back again ignites, sending him back toward the plane. He slams into the wing supports, shuts the pack off and grabs his unconscious friend, wrenching him free of the plane.

As the plane hits the ground and explodes in a fiery ball, Cliff sweeps close to the ground and deposits the pilot safely atop a large in-flated balloon, from which he is pulled by concerned onlookers on the ground.

Once again zooming into the air, Cliff flies through the clouds and pulls parallel to a passenger plane. He raises his hand in a salute to the startled passengers, unwittingly switching off his jet pack. He spirals toward the ground, regaining power at the last moment. He zips wildly close to the ground, through corn stalks, laundry lines and fruit orchards, and skips like a rock across the surface of a pond.

Finally coming to a panting stop at the edge of the pond, Cliff yanks his helmet off, shakes his head vigorously and exclaims, "I *like* it!"

That's exactly what it's like when God makes a person holy—isn't it? At least that's what a lot of people expect. They imagine the initial experience of holiness to be accompanied by some great commotion or sign. They anticipate "great balls of fire," an explosion of emotion.

As a matter of fact, some people do experience a moment of great emotion, when their souls are visited by the Holy Spirit of God in a way they had never before experienced. But that is not always the case, and for some people the expectation of an emotional experience becomes an obstacle to holiness. They take the steps to the vertical lifestyle, but when they don't experience fireworks in their souls or bombs bursting in their hearts, they assume that God won't—or can't—break the power of sin in their lives.

But such a tragic mistake can be avoided if you understand that God may accept the offering of your consecrated heart to the accompaniment of a brass band, with cymbals clashing, trumpets blaring and timpani pounding in your soul . . . but He may not. Either way, He can still "sanctify you through and through" (1 Thessalonians 5:23).

Everyone begins the vertical life in a different way. Some are "knocked off their horses," sort of like Paul when he first met the risen Christ. Others experience something more like the "gentle whisper" Elijah heard on the mountain of God. Still others begin to live in the vertical with no apparent response or confirmation from God other than the moment-by-moment deliverance from sin that they experience.

That's the way it is most often, it seems; the vertical life begins not like a mighty explosion, but like a small, silent spark that grows brighter and warmer with every passing moment.

Word Up

Learn more about the vertical life by taking the time to thoughtfully and prayerfully consider the following:

- Read Isaiah 32:17. What do you think this verse means? (check all that apply)

  __righteousness is never exuberant or loud
  __living "vertically" means always speaking in whispers
  __holiness brings an enduring quietness in a person's heart
  __a person who's living the vertical lifestyle could never be a cheerleader
  ✓righteousness brings blessings, both to a nation and to individuals

- Questions for thought: Do you find yourself reluctant to live in the vertical? Why? Is it because any of the obstacles to vertical living mentioned in this book present a problem for you? Which ones? Do you face obstacles not mentioned? What are they? If the answer to any of these questions was yes, take a few moments to present them to God in prayer, asking for His help in dealing honestly and sincerely with them.

I don't really have a problem w/ living in the vertical. It's just what the devil is always there to step in when I least expect it and it seems there's nothing I can do about it

The Steps to
Vertical Living

18

The Danger Zone

*S*arai finished scraping a dirty plate into the garbage disposal: the yawning mouth of her husband's nephew, Lot (who got his name because he sure could eat a lot).

"There you are!" she said as her husband, Abram, entered the tent. "You're two hours late for dinner and you can't even pick up a ram's horn and call?"

"Sarai," Abram said breathlessly, ignoring her flashing eyes. "I have some wonderful news!"

"Unless Ed McMahon's waiting outside with a check from Patriarch's Clearinghouse Sweepstakes, I don't want to hear it."

"Just listen, will you?" He gripped Sarai's shoulders in his hands and peered, wild-eyed, into her face. "The Lord spoke to me today."

"Oy!" she wailed. "This isn't gonna be another one of your schemes, is it, Abram? Because we still have 5,000 boxes of M&Ms to sell." She pointed to a stack of cardboard boxes in the corner of the tent. " 'We can win a giant-screen TV,' you said, but where would we plug it in, Abram, huh? And I have to watch those M&Ms like a hawk, or the only thing left of them would be a chocolate ring around Lot's mouth!"

"Just hear me out, woman," Abram said. "The Lord spoke to me today, and he said, 'Leave your country, your people and your father's household and go to the land I will show you.' "

"Oy!" Sarai shouted. "You can't be serious!"

"He said, 'I will make you into a great nation and I will bless you; I will make your name great, and you will be a blessing.' "

"Blessing schmessing! What about me, Mister I'm-gonna-be-a-great-nation? Did you ever think to ask me what I want? Did you ever think to ask if I want to leave my ladies' club and my hairdresser? And what about Lot? He'd have to change schools!"

"He doesn't go to school, dear," Abram sighed. "This is the 19th century B.C., remember?"

"I don't care." She plopped down onto the fancy rug and pillows of the tent and folded her arms in a gesture of stubbornness. "I'm not moving from this spot."

Sarai's not alone; a lot of people hate to move. But even if she hadn't hated moving, she probably still would have balked at Abram's proposal because he wasn't just asking her to move; he was asking her to move out of her "comfort zone" and into the "danger zone."

Imagine God asking you to leave the only place you've ever lived, the only people you've ever known, the only family you've ever had, to follow Him to "the land I will show you" (Genesis 12:1). Imagine Him telling you to pack your bags, and say goodbye to everything—your school, your friends, the mall—and head down the road without even knowing where the next McDonald's is or where you're supposed to stop. If you don't know where you're going, how would you even know when you got there?

That's what God asked Abram to do. He told him to leave his comfort zone and head right into the danger zone. And, amazingly, Abram did it.

That's what God asks you to do, too, if you want to experience the vertical lifestyle. Some of the steps you must take to be "wholly sanctified" (see 1 Thessalonians 5:23, KJV) may be scary, like taking a step into the unknown. It can be a bit like going out on a blind date or signing up for a mission trip; you're not sure what's going to happen or whether you're going to like it.

But if you're serious about living in the vertical (and, if you've made it this far in this book, you *must* be serious!), you will probably have to step out of your comfort zone and into the danger zone, a place you've never been before. You'll take steps you've never taken before, make commitments you've never made before and break deep-seated patterns you've never even questioned before.

Of course, you can always stay where you're comfortable and risk becoming a "spiritual couch potato." Or you can enter the danger zone and risk becoming a spiritual Indiana Jones. It's your call, but you probably already know which choice God wants you to make.

Word Up

Give further thought to your entry into the danger zone by completing the following:

- Read Hebrews 11:8-19, which talks a little more about Abram (later Abraham) and his entry into the danger zone. What three changes did Abraham face as a result of following God into the danger zone?

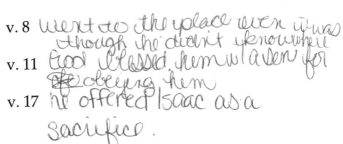

v. 8 Went to the place even if was though he didn't know where

v. 11 God blessed him w/ a son for obeying him

v. 17 he offered Isaac as a sacrifice.

- What was the result(s) of Abraham's entry into the danger zone? (check all that apply)

  __He became the founder of a world religion
  __He had seven sons
  ✓He became the friend of God
  __He became President of the United States
  __He became the father of many nations
  __He became the laughingstock of his friends and family

- What do you fear most about following God into the danger zone of radical commitment and vertical living?

people well laugh at me and I wont be able to have fun anymore.

Take a moment to tell God about your fear and commit it to Him in prayer.

19

Life-O-Suction

"Did you hear about Jeanine?" Carrie Deway gripped her best friend, Anna Wawego, by the elbow.

"Hear what?" Anna asked, facing her friend in the school hallway.

"She did it!"

"Did what?"

"You know," Carrie insisted, rolling her eyes.

"I do not," Anna said, shifting her tiny book bag from one shoulder to the other. "What are you talking about?"

"She said she was thinking about getting liposuction on her thighs, remember?"

Anna shook her head. "Liposuction?"

"You know," Carrie repeated, "where they cut a hole in you and take, like, a vacuum cleaner hose and suck out your fat?"

"Oh," Anna said. "I remember something about that."

"Well, she did it! I can't believe it, but she did it! She won't be back in school for a few more days. You want to go to her house?"

Anna stopped and tilted her head slightly. "Yeah, that would be nice."

"Now, when we get there, if her legs are covered up, you distract her and I'll figure out a way to yank the covers so we can see how much fat they took out, and then—ow!"

Anna whacked the back of her friend's head with her Western Civ. book.

"What did you do that for?" Carrie asked, rubbing her head and flashing a hurt look at Anna.

Anna didn't answer but shook her head. "I think you need a little liposuction done on that fat head of yours," she said.

Carrie's not the only one who could benefit from a little unconventional liposuction. Actually, it's not liposuction that we need; it's "life-o-suction." In a way, that's the first step toward vertical living, a kind of spiritual liposuction that begins with *heartfelt confession.*

If you would be holy, if you want a life of close communion with God, a life of victory over sin, you must begin with a prayer like that of David:

Search me, O God, and know my heart;
    test me and know my anxious

thoughts.
See if there is any offensive way in me,
and lead me in the way everlasting.
(Psalm 139:23-24)

With the help of God's Spirit, you must search your heart for anything—any act, any attitude, any affection—that is offensive to God.

Like a bloodhound sniffing a trail, you must ruthlessly search and identify any sinful *acts*. You must ask yourself such questions as, "Have I lied or lusted? Have I hurt or cheated anyone? Have I done things I shouldn't, or left undone things I should do?"

You must examine your *attitudes*, asking, "Am I harboring hatred or rebellion in my heart? Am I nursing a spirit of jealousy or pride? Am I unwilling to forgive someone? Am I unable to love someone?"

You must also confront your *affections*, asking, "Do I love things that God hates? Do I treasure anything above God? Do I tolerate affinities or affiliations that would offend God?"

When you have so examined your soul, you can then confess to God any "offensive way" that is in you, and proceed to the next step to vertical living, which is *cleansing*.

Native Americans had a custom many years ago, which they performed whenever a white child or young person was taken prisoner. It was a ceremony by which that child was officially adopted into the tribe. The tribe would take the captive to a river or lake, and there several members of the tribe would take stiff brushes and coarse rags and begin to vigorously scrub the skin of the captive.

Finally, when the child's skin had been rubbed nearly raw, the ceremony was completed. It was thought that, in this way, the "white" had been rubbed from the person's skin and, therefore, out of his or her soul. From that time on, the child was considered a full-blooded member of the tribe. That washing had provided a new start; in the eyes of the tribe, his or her past was completely gone.

That is the sort of thing God promises to the young man or woman who will confess all unforgiven sin and seek a new start. Again, it can begin with a prayer like that of David:

> Wash away all my iniquity
> and cleanse me from my sin. . . .
> Cleanse me with hyssop, and I will be
> clean;
> wash me, and I will be whiter than
> snow. . . .
> Create in me a pure heart, O God,
> and renew a steadfast spirit within
> me. (Psalm 51:2, 7, 10)

It doesn't matter if your life has been one long history of sin and ungodliness; it doesn't matter if your life to this point has been spent largely ignoring God; it doesn't matter that your life up till now has been one continuous string of coming to God and then sinning, coming to God and then sinning some more; it doesn't matter that your life so far has been inconsistent, unstable and without direction.

God can give you "life-o-suction!" He can enter your sin-stained heart and clean it out entirely, giving you a fresh start. All you need to do is to confess your sins and then ask Him to forgive them, ask Him to cleanse you, ask Him to start you on "the Way of Holiness" (Isaiah 35:8).

Word Up

The book of First John in the Bible has a few things to say about the process of "life-o-suction." Complete the following and then check your answers by reading the corresponding verses: (circle your answers)

1. "If we claim to be without sin . . ." (1 John 1:8)
    a. We can get away with a lot more
    b. We deceive ourselves
    c. We are eligible to be elders in the church
    d. We can teach the junior high Sunday school class

2. "If we confess our sins . . ." (1 John 1:9)

    a. Other people will look down on us
    b. God will never let us live it down

    c. We can impress others with how rotten we were before we came to Christ

    d. God will forgive our sins and purify us from all unrighteousness

3. "You know that [Christ] appeared so that . . ." (1 John 3:5)

    a. He might take away our sins

    b. We would have something to do on Sundays

    c. Ministers might have jobs

    d. We would know what He looked like

- Have you experienced "life-o-suction?" Has your heart been cleansed of all sin by the power of God? If not, pray Psalm 51:1-12 out loud to God, making it truly the prayer of your heart.

20

Dead or Alive

*J*esse James robbed banks and trains throughout Missouri and neighboring states for much
of two decades. He and his brother Frank rode a
murderous outlaw trail in the 1860s and 1870s.

But his trail came to an end in 1882. Missouri governor Thomas T. Crittenden issued an offer for a $10,000 reward for the capture of Frank and Jesse James—and a promise to go easy on any gang member who would supply information leading to the outlaws' arrest.

Bob Ford, a newcomer to the James gang, met with the governor and proposed that, if the terms of the capture were "dead or alive," he and his brother Charley would deliver the feared outlaw. The governor agreed.

On the morning of April 3, 1882, Bob and Charley Ford were in Jesse's home in St. Joseph, Missouri, where Jesse lived with his wife and children under an assumed name. Jesse pulled off his coat and pistols and stepped onto a chair to dust a picture. Bob Ford drew his gun and, from less than four feet away, shot Jesse James in the back of the head. The Ford brothers quickly collected the "dead or alive" reward money.

Not very nice, huh? But some would argue that it had to be done. In any case, it's more than a page in one of those "Outlaws of the Wild West" books you see advertised on TV. It's also a fitting illustration of an important step to the vertical life.

Now, don't go out looking for an outlaw to "plug" in the back of the head; what Bob Ford did to Jesse James is kind of what you must do to self and sin. The Bible puts it this way:

In the same way, count yourselves dead to sin but alive to God in Christ Jesus. Therefore do not let sin reign in your mortal body so that you obey its evil desires. Do not offer the parts of your body to sin, as instruments of wickedness, but rather offer yourselves to God, as those who have been brought from death to life; and offer the parts of your body to him as instruments of righteousness. For sin shall not be your master, because you are not under law, but under grace. (Romans 6:11-14)

In other words, a crucial step to living a life of victory and joy is to pronounce your old self D.O.A. (dead on arrival), and consider your life to be no longer your own, but Christ's. Or, to use one poet's imagery:

Once there lived another man within me,
    Child of earth and slave of Satan, he;
But I nailed him to the cross of Jesus,
    And that man is nothing now to me.
Now Another Man is living in me,
    And I count His blessed life as mine;
I have died with Him to all my own life;
    I have ris'n to all His life divine.

That is exactly what the Word of God says in the sixth chapter of Romans. In that brief chapter, the apostle Paul reveals a purpose, a process and a promise.

The Purpose. The Bible says in Romans 6:6 that "our old self was crucified with [Christ] so that the body of sin might be done away with, *that we should no longer be slaves to sin*" (emphasis added). Jesus' triumphant work on the cross and His resurrection from the dead dealt a deathblow to sin! That, in a nutshell, is the very purpose for which Christ came: "that he might destroy the works of the devil" (1 John 3:8, KJV). He came to destroy the devil's work—not to hinder them, not to cripple them, but to *destroy* them. His purpose in coming was "that the body of sin [in you!] might be done away with" (Romans 6:6)—not subdued, not reduced, but *powerless!*

The Process. If it is true that our Savior is capable of destroying the works of the devil, of ruining the power of sin, how does that happen? How does it become a reality? By the process Paul describes in verse 11 of Romans 6: "Count yourselves dead to sin but alive to God in Christ Jesus." It's a two-step process. First, you count yourself dead to sin. You decide to *believe* that what the Bible says is true (that is, that you are in fact dead to sin) and, like a father who disowns and disinherits his son, you determine to *act* as though sin no longer exists for you. Second, you count yourself alive to God in Christ Jesus. That means the "old you"—the one who thought all those awful things, did all those rotten things and said all those horrible things—is dead and buried, just like Jesus was buried; the "new you," however, is alive to God—interested in the things of God, able to follow the way of God and sharing in the very nature of God (2 Peter 1:4). But this process can only be done by someone who is *in Christ Jesus*, because it involves, not an exercise of your will power, but the exercise of His Spirit's power.

The Promise. The promise Paul makes in Romans 6 is so straightforward, you can hardly mistake it, though many people stumble over it, avoid it or explain it away—perhaps because it offers a promise that is not a reality in their lives, and so they conclude that it cannot mean what it says. Romans 6:14 says, "Sin shall not be your master." Some people teach and behave as though Paul had said, "Sin *eventually* shall not be your master." Others think Paul must have meant, "*Generally speaking,* sin shall not be your master." But the promise is pretty clear: "Sin shall not be your master" . . . not mostly, not generally, not eventually, but definitely, specifically, currently.

The secret is in consciously and constantly—through the Spirit of Christ Himself—counting yourself dead to sin and self and alive to God. It means nailing your sin-bound life to the cross and allowing God to raise you with Christ in a new, heaven-bound life. It means simply to stop living horizontally and begin to live vertically.

Does it sound too good to be true?

You have God's word on the matter.

Word Up

Are you dead or alive to sin and self? Take a few moments to answer that question by completing the following:

• Place a check mark beside any question you can honestly answer, "yes."

___Has God forgiven your sins through Jesus Christ? "He himself bore our sins in his body on the tree, so that we might die to sins and live for righteousness" (1 Peter 2:24).

___Have you "received Christ Jesus as Lord?" Then "you died, and your life is now hidden with Christ in God" (Colossians 2:6, 3:3).

___Does Jesus live in your heart by faith? "I have been crucified with Christ and I no longer live, but Christ lives in me" (Galatians 2:20).

___Do you belong to Christ Jesus? "Those who belong to Christ Jesus have crucified the sinful nature with its passions and desires" (Galatians 5:24).

__Have you been raised with Christ (into new life as a Christian)? "Since, then, you have been raised with Christ, . . . set your hearts on things above" (Colossians 3:1).

__Have you counted yourself dead to sin and alive to God in Christ? "For we know that our old self was crucified with him so that the body of sin might be done away with, that we should no longer be slaves to sin" (Romans 6:6).

- If you have answered "yes" to all the above, take a moment to thank God for His promise that "sin shall not be your master" (Romans 6:14). If you did not answer "yes" to all the above, review those questions that are not checked; you can make each one true by breathing a simple, sincere prayer to God, asking Him to perform that work in your life.

21

Holy Cow

The high priest, a white-haired man with a full white beard and large, callused hands, strode to the temple, his face grim. He wore layers of thick, expensive robes and a colorful ephod, an apron-like garment secured at the shoulders and tied by a thick sash around his ample waist. From his shoulders hung a jeweled breastpiece.

Each of his hands gripped two legs of a young bull slung across his shoulders. With the priest's every step, the bull bleated and brayed like a dozen angry animals. As the man approached the temple with his offering, the animal smelled the blood and flesh of past sacrifices, and its eyes widened with brute fear.

The priest washed his hands at a huge basin

at the southeast corner of the temple as two other priests ceremoniously washed the animal in a smaller basin on the opposite side of the temple steps.

Finally, after the throat of the young bull had been slit and the blood smeared on the four corners of the altar of burnt offering, the priest climbed the wide steps to the altar of burnt offering, where a wood fire blazed, and gingerly—as if setting a holiday table—arranged the animal on the altar, where it would burn all that day and through the coming night.

That burnt offering from the high priest—like all the offerings God commanded in the Old Testament—was considered holy. It was just an animal, an animal that smelled bad and chewed cud, no less! Yet God said that "such an animal given to the Lord becomes holy" (Leviticus 27:9).

Did that mean that an animal can become morally superior to you and me? Did it mean that the creature to be sacrificed had some spiritual quality that made it holy? Did it mean that the beast went to heaven when it died? No.

No? Well, then, how could a cud-chewing, grass-eating, foul-smelling, fly-drawing critter become holy? *Because it belonged only—and completely—to God.*

God declared that anything—or anyone—that was set apart completely for God, that was never again to be used for any purpose except

for Him, was "holy." It was said to be "sanctified," set apart for God's purposes. In this way,
the temple was holy. The altar was holy. The
furniture of the temple was holy. The offerings,
whether animal or grain or liquid, were holy.

Only that which belongs completely—and
only—to God can be holy. Or, to put it in other
words, only that which is consecrated can be
sanctified. Or, to put it in the language we've
been using throughout this book, an important
step to vertical living is *unconditional surrender*.

In military terms, unconditional surrender is
giving up on a battle or a war and *giving in* to
the opponent without any demands or conditions. In spiritual terms, unconditional surrender is giving up your life, your self, your time,
your talents, your possessions, your ambitions—even your favorite sins—and giving in
to God's loving authority over your life. It is not
giving up on yourself, but giving yourself to
God. It is not giving up on life, but giving your
life to God. It is not giving up on success, but
giving your desire for success to God. It is not
giving up on pleasure, but giving all your
pleasures to God.

The young man or woman who surrenders
to God—who gives himself or herself completely to God, no questions asked, with nothing withheld, no conditions, no demands, no
"escape clause"—will suddenly and certainly
discover a new usefulness and effectiveness, a
new vibrancy and vitality to his or her life.

Just as a horse will only begin to win races after it surrenders to the rider; just as a lump of clay only becomes a treasure after it surrenders to the potter; just as a violin only makes beautiful music after it surrenders to the virtuoso's touch; so you will only begin to experience fulfillment, joy, peace and victory after you completely—and unconditionally—surrender to God.

Then you will begin to know what it's like to live in the vertical, because "everything [that is] so devoted is most holy to the LORD" (Leviticus 27:28).

Word Up

Discover more about the holiness bestowed by God upon things or people that belong only to Him by completing the following:

- Read the following verses and, in the space provided, write what God called holy:

  Psalm 20:6
  Leviticus 27:14, 16
  Exodus 29:42-43
  Psalm 2:6
  Exodus 29:36-37

- Why did God call these things holy?

- Have you surrendered unconditionally to God? Have you given up your life, your self, your time, talents, possessions, ambitions— even your favorite sins—and given yourself completely to God and His loving authority over your life? If you haven't, consider praying a prayer something like this:

Father, I want to know You in Your fullness; I want to be wholly consecrated to You. Right now, with all my heart, I surrender completely to You—no questions asked, no conditions, nothing withheld, no demands, no "escape clause." I give all to You: my life, my self, my time, talents, possessions, ambitions. I give all that I am, all that I have, all that I value, all that I hope, to You. Please take my offering and do whatever You choose with it. I trust You with it all. In Jesus' name, amen.

22

Run with the One That Brung Ya

*C*lem and Cadiddle Hopper sat rocking on the front porch of their cabin, waiting for their 16-year-old daughter, Clementine, to come home after the church picnic. Clem cleaned his varmint gun while Cadiddle, his wife of 18 years, sewed on the patchwork wedding dress she hoped Clementine would someday wear.

Suddenly, the coughing and clacking sound of Wilferd Platt's truck announced the arrival of Clementine and the first boy ever to take her to the church picnic. As Clem and Cadiddle watched, however, their daughter climbed out of the truck, turned toward the house and stomped up the steps as Wilferd Platt drove away.

"What's the matter, darlin'?" Cadiddle asked, but her daughter simply stormed past her and into the cabin.

Cadiddle followed and sat on the bed beside Clementine, who lay face down in her pillow, crying like a cow being milked without gloves on a cold January morning.

"Wilferd said he never wanted to take me to a church picnic agin!" she sobbed.

"What fer?" Cadiddle asked.

"Just because I run the three-legged race with Bubby McAllister," she said, and buried her face again in the pillow.

"Oh, my darling Clementine," her mother sighed. "Ya mean to tell me that Wilferd Platt brung ya to the picnic, and ya throwed him over fer Bubby McAllister?"

Clementine snuffed loudly and wiped her nose on the long sleeve of her dress. "I didn't throw him over," she protested. "I just run with Bubby, that's all."

Cadiddle wrapped her arms around her daughter and began to rock her back and forth on the bed like a baby. "It's my fault, darlin'," she said. "It's my fault. I shoulda told ya. I shoulda told ya."

"Told me what, Mama?"

"I shoulda told ya the number one rule for goin' to a church picnic with a boy," she said.

Clementine wiped her nose on her sleeve again, and her mother rolled her eyes. "Don't use your sleeve for that," she scolded. "Use the edge of the bedcovers."

Clementine nodded and lifted the bedspread to her nose. "What's the number one rule for going to a church picnic with a boy?" she asked her mother.

"Run with the one that brung ya," she answered. "If'n a boy brung ya to the picnic, ya set beside him fer the pie-eatin' contest. If'n a boy brung ya, ya use his varmint gun fer the tin can-shootin' contest. And most important, ya *shore* run the three-legged race with the one that brung ya. Or you're liable not to get brung agin."

Cadiddle Hopper's rule isn't only wise counsel for church picnics; it's a key step to the vertical life.

A lot of people who have experienced salvation through faith in Christ make the same mistake young Clementine Hopper made. They develop the mistaken impression that sanctification is achieved through a process much different than the process that brought them salvation. They believe that holiness comes through practice, that righteousness can be developed through effort, that they can obtain victory over sin by clever gimmicks or creative techniques. The number one rule of vertical living, however, is to "run with the one that brung ya."

That means you must come to Christ in simple, childlike faith, as you did when you first sought forgiveness for your sins and salvation from "the wages of sin" (Romans 6:23). It means to depend, not on anything you may do, but on His grace, for "it is by grace you have been saved, through faith—and this not from yourselves, it is the gift of God—not by works, so that no one can boast" (Ephesians 2:8-9). It means to trust God for your sanctification, just as you trusted Him for your salvation, "because [you] know whom [you] have believed, and [are] convinced that he is able to guard what [you] have entrusted to him" (2 Timothy 1:12).

As Paul wrote,

[J]ust as you received Christ Jesus as Lord, continue to live in him, rooted and built up in him, strengthened in the faith as you were taught, and overflowing with thankfulness. (Colossians 2:6-7)

The vertical life, from beginning to end, is "by grace . . . through faith" (Ephesians 2:8). Or, as Cadiddle Hopper might put it, it was faith in Jesus that brung you; that same faith in Jesus ought to be your partner for the whole picnic.

Word Up

Explore what it means to be *kept* by faith in Jesus Christ by completing the following:

- Read Hebrews 12:1-2. What do you think this verse means by calling Jesus "the *author* . . . of our faith?"

- What do you think that verse means by referring to Jesus as "the . . . *perfecter* of our faith?"

- Read First Peter 1:3-5. How do these verses say we are "shielded" (NIV) or "kept" (KJV)?

  through

  by

- Take a few minutes to pray First Peter 1:3-5, substituting "my" and "me" for "our" and "you."

- Have you placed your faith in Christ as Savior? Have you placed your faith in Christ as Sanctifier? If you answered no to either question, take time right now to pray and place your faith fully in Him.

23

Inner Space

A man in a lab coat stumbles off the elevator and collapses into Jack Putter's arms. Jack doesn't know that the man is a scientist who has just succeeded in a top-secret attempt to shrink a human test pilot and his "spacecraft" to microscopic size. Jack doesn't know that a dangerous spy has just shot the scientist. Jack doesn't know that the scientist holds in his hand the syringe that contains the germ-sized astronaut. He only feels a sharp stab when the scientist injects the contents of the syringe into Jack's bloodstream.

Lt. Tuck Pendleton, the test pilot who expected to be injected into the bloodstream of a caged rabbit in the top-secret laboratory, soon discovers that he has been introduced into the body of a hypochondriac grocery clerk who suffers from nightmares, numerous allergies and a crippling case of nerves. Over the course of the next several hours, Jack discovers that his body is inhabited by an impetuous, swaggering pilot who thrives on adventure and likes to make up his own rules.

At the prompting of Pendleton, who can see through Jack's eyes and hear through his ears, Jack begins to do things he would never have done without Pendleton's voice in his ears. He wrestles a gun away from one of the bad guys and knocks the man out with a blow to the back of the head. He dives out the back of a moving panel truck where he was being held prisoner, swings from the door and jumps into a passing car. He throws a knockout punch to one of the bad guys and ties him up in the bathtub. Jack Putter, under Pendleton's influence, is transformed into a swashbuckling, self-confident hero, capable of things he never before dreamed possible.

That fantastic scenario forms the plot of Steven Spielberg's 1987 movie, *Inner Space*, starring Dennis Quaid as Tuck Pendleton and Martin Short as Jack Putter. It also resembles the vertical life.

The young man or woman who has experienced new life in Christ receives, at the moment of rebirth, the Holy Spirit. Christ Himself, through the Holy Spirit, comes to live inside the new believer. "On that day you will realize that I am in my Father, and you are in me, and I am in you" (John 14:20).

If you have received forgiveness of sins and salvation through Jesus Christ, you have something infinitely better than a courageous test pilot living inside you—you have Christ Himself!

Living in you is the crucified Christ, who "died to sin once for all" (Romans 6:10). Living in you is the risen Christ, who "was raised from the dead through the glory of the Father [so that] we too may live a new life" (6:4). Living in you is the reigning Christ, "who has become. . . *our* righteousness, holiness and redemption" (1 Corinthians 1:30).

Christ is your holiness. The Spirit of Christ, who lives in you, is righteous; therefore, you don't have to be righteous, you can let *Him* be righteous *in you*. The *Holy* Spirit of God indwells you through the work of Jesus Christ; therefore, you don't have to be holy, you can let *Him* be holy *in you*. The power of God has given you everything you need for life and godliness; therefore, you don't have to imitate God, you already "participate in the divine nature," which enables you to "escape the corruption in the world [that is] caused by evil desires" (2 Peter 1:4).

Strictly speaking, then, sanctification is not something *you* achieve; it is something Christ achieves in you. Holiness is not something *you* acquire; it is something already possessed by Christ, who lives in you. The vertical life is not something *you* do; it is the life of Christ being lived through you.

"I have been crucified with Christ," Paul testified, "and I no longer live, but Christ lives in me" (Galatians 2:20). *That* is vertical living.

Do you remember the scene in *The Wizard of Oz* when Dorothy's dog, Toto, yanks the curtain aside and reveals that the words and actions of the "mighty" wizard were controlled by a man working buttons and levers behind the screen? Well, if we could yank some spiritual curtain aside to reveal the secrets of godly men and women through the centuries—"who through faith conquered kingdoms, administered justice, and gained what was promised; who shut the mouths of lions, quenched the fury of the flames, and escaped the edge of the sword; whose weakness was turned to strength" (Hebrews 11:33-34)—we would discover that they had no holiness, no righteousness of their own, but that they were controlled by the Spirit of Christ, living His holy life through them.

Living in the vertical is nothing more—and nothing less—than allowing Christ to live in you, pushing the buttons and pulling the levers of your life, day by day and moment by moment.

Word Up

Take a few moments to learn more by completing the following:

• Unscramble the bold-faced words in the following verses of Scripture to determine what they say about whether a pure life is possible and, if so, how it comes about:

And if the **ripits** of him who **sidare** Jesus
from the dead is living in you, he who
sidare Christ from the dead will also
give life to your **trolam** bodies through his
ripits, who lives in you. (Romans 8:11)

And this is my prayer: that your love may
bodnau more and more in **lowdekeng**
and depth of **sinthig**, so that you may be
able to discern what is best and may be
rupe and **saleblems** until the day of
Christ, filled with the **rufit** of
snereoussight that comes through Jesus
Christ—to the glory and praise of God.
(Philippians 1:9-11)

- Are you allowing Christ to "push the buttons"
and "pull the levers" in *your* life? If not, why?

  If you're willing to allow Him to completely control you from the inside out, spend a few moments in prayer to tell Him that. (The next
  chapters will further explain how to let Christ
  control you.)

24

Holy Joe

*Y*oung Joe sat on the edge of the cot in his jail cell, and nodded at the dirty, toothless man who sat on the other bunk, leaning against the cold wall of the tiny cell.

"What are you in for?" Joe asked.

The grizzled prisoner coughed and spat. "I stole a chariot." He coughed again. "Took it to a chop shop. Almost had it stripped when they busted in. Five more minutes, the evidence would've been gone." The man eyed his young cell mate. "You?"

Joseph sighed. "Attempted rape. But I didn't do it."

"Yeah," the man said, flashing a knowing smile. "Me neither."

"No, I really didn't. See, I worked for

Potiphar."

"Potiphar!" the man straightened himself and perched on the edge of his cot. "The captain of the guard?"

Joe nodded. "Anyway, his wife started putting the moves on me."

The man rubbed his filthy hands together. "This is getting good."

"She wanted me to go to bed with her."

"Wait a minute, you're talking about Potiphar's wife, the one who does that jeans commercial, right? She's a fox!"

Joe shrugged. "Yeah, I guess so. Anyway—"

"You lucky dog!"

Joe shook his head vigorously. "No, you don't get it. I never touched her."

"You what?"

"I didn't go to bed with her. She wanted me to, but when I refused, she kept after me. Finally," he said, his voice dropping, "I guess she got mad and framed me for attempted rape."

The man coughed and spat again. "Let me get this straight," he said. "You could have gone to bed with the foxiest woman since Marcia Brady and you passed? Why?"

"I couldn't! It would have been a sin against God."

"You mean a gorgeous girl throws herself at you, and you just say no?"

Joe nodded, and the man looked like he was about to have a heart attack. "Weren't you even tempted?"

"Well, sure," Joe said. "I guess so, but God was with me the whole time. He just kinda handled it for me."

Joe attributed his "escape from the corruption in the world [that is] caused by evil desires" to his constant fellowship with God. The Bible puts it this way: "the LORD was with Joseph and gave him success in whatever he did" (Genesis 39:23; see also Genesis 39:2, 39:21, 41:38). That's a key part of living in the vertical.

Some people—who experience a clean heart through the power of the Holy Spirit and die to sin and self through their identification with Jesus Christ and consecrate themselves wholly to God, that through faith they might be "filled with the fruit of righteousness that comes through Jesus Christ" (Philippians 1:11)—still fail to live the vertical life because they do not "abide" in Christ.

"No one who abides in [Christ] sins," the Bible says (1 John 3:6, NASB). The Greek word for "abides" in that verse is *meno,* and it is translated into English by many different words (remain, endure, dwell, continue, abide, etc.). Abiding in Christ, however, is not complicated; it is simply remaining in God's company and cultivating a constant fellowship with Him.

How do you do that? Obviously, constant fellowship with God will involve *prayer.* You must develop a habit of prayer, preferably at the beginning of each day, in which you offer praise to God, submit yourself (and your needs) to Him, and spend time in prayer for others. But the mistake many people make is to let their praying end when their "prayer time" ends. God's Word commands you to "pray without ceasing" (1 Thessalonians 5:17, KJV); you must make communion with God a moment-by-moment experience, so that when temptation comes, you can say (like Joseph), "God was with me the whole time and He just kinda handled it for me."

Constant fellowship with God also involves *Bible reading and Bible study*. Fellowship with God is a two-way street. You wouldn't think of calling your boyfriend or girlfriend on the phone, talking for an hour or two and then hanging up without letting him (or her) say a word, would you? Of course not, because in any loving relationship there will be things you want to *hear* as well as things you want to *say*. Your relationship with God is no different. Reading His Word allows Him to speak to *you*, to tell you He loves you, to tell you how you can please Him and how He can bless you; studying the Bible (which is not the same as reading it) allows Him to instruct you, to teach you His promises and precepts and fill you with "the mind of Christ" (1 Corinthians 2:16, KJV).

Finally, constant fellowship with God will require *regular worship and fellowship with other believers*. "Let us not give up meeting together," the Bible says, "as some are in the habit of doing, but let us encourage one another" (Hebrews 10:25). A habit of regular worship with other Christians and fellowship with believers who can encourage you in your walk with God are key ingredients of the vertical life.

If you cultivate such practices and make them as much a part of your daily routine as blinking and breathing, you will prove the truth of Jesus' promise:

> Remain in me, and I will remain in you. No branch can bear fruit by itself; it must remain in the vine. Neither can you bear fruit unless you remain in me. . . . Apart from me you can do nothing. (John 15:4-5)

Word Up

- A famous book bears the title, *The Practice of the Presence of God*, a phrase that refers to the habit of constant fellowship. Can you think of any ways (in addition to the three mentioned in the chapter above) that you can begin to practice the presence of God? List them below:

- If you wish to develop a habit of constant fellowship with God, begin now by praying this (or a similar) prayer (based on *The Practice of the Presence of God*):

Father, help me, please, by Your Holy Spirit, to "exercise" myself in the knowledge and love of God, to endeavor to live in a continual sense of Your presence and, if possible, never to forget or neglect You even for a moment.

Help me to fill my mind with prayer and Your Word and to fill my heart with worship and fellowship, so that when I go to school or work or out with friends, I will be in Your presence no less than when I am in church or in private prayer. I commit myself today to the practice of Your presence. In Jesus' name, amen.

25

Ryan's Repentance

𝒯hree-year-old Ryan played in the back yard
with his brother, Matt. Suddenly, the two sib-
lings had a disagreement about who would get to

shoot the Super-Duper Drencher Gun and who would be drenched. When Matt gripped the gun and ripped it out of Ryan's hands, Ryan slugged his brother in the head.

Suddenly, *immediately*, before his brother's first cries of pain were heard, Ryan flashed a panicked glance toward his house and bolted inside, not to hide, but to run sobbing into his father's arms.

"I'm really sorry, Daddy. I'm really, really sorry."

By the time Matt stumbled groggily into the house, Ryan had fully confessed his crime and repented of his wrongdoing. His father still disciplined his son, but Ryan's quick action shortened his agony and probably lessened his penalty.

Ryan's repentance can teach us quite a bit about the vertical life. Vertical living does not mean the devil will never again accuse you of sin. As the apostle John wrote, "My dear children, I write this to you so that you will not sin. But if anybody does sin, we have one who speaks to the Father in our defense—Jesus Christ, the Righteous One" (1 John 2:1).

As chapter 14 mentioned, the vertical life does not make it impossible for you to sin; it makes it possible for you *not* to sin.

An important step to victory is "keeping short accounts" with God. You see, just as there are advantages to paying bills the moment they're received (such as saving interest, decreasing the likelihood of losing or forgetting the bill, avoiding late fees, easier record-keeping, etc.) there are huge benefits to responding like Ryan when you stumble into sin or error.

The classic, *The Practice of the Presence of God*, mentioned in the last chapter, relates how Brother Lawrence, the 17th-century Christian who cultivated constant fellowship with God, used Ryan's technique in keeping his soul clean:

> When he had finished his work for the day, he examined himself and evaluated how he had done in obeying God and staying in fellowship with him. If he had enjoyed victory over sin and remained in fellowship with God, he returned thanks to God. If he had sinned or failed, he asked for God's forgiveness. Then, without being discouraged, he set his mind right again, and continued his practice of the presence of God, as if he had never deviated from it. "That way," he said, "by immediately repenting after my falls, and being immediately restored to fellowship with God, I have come to the point where it would be as difficult for me *not* to think of God as it was at first to remain aware of Him.

If you're living in the vertical, you need not despair if the tempter obtains a momentary victory over you; the solution is to run immediately to your Father's arms, seeking forgiveness and restoration and then (like Ryan) go back "outside" to play, more aware of the Father's love and grace and watchful presence.

Word Up

Take a few moments to confirm the message of this chapter by completing the following:

- How do you tend to react when you sin or fail? (check all that apply)

  __I give up
  __I decide to try harder
  __I lock myself into a closet and eat Oreos until I'm sick
  __I get depressed
  __I don't let it bother me
  __I run immediately to my Father's arms, seeking forgiveness and restoration and then (like Ryan) go back "outside" to play, more aware of the Father's love and grace and watchful presence.

- How will you react from now on? (circle any of the above choices that apply)

- If you have decided to imitate Ryan's repentance from now on, consider praying the following prayer (or one like it):

  Father, I know that Your will is that I do not sin. But I thank You that, if I do, I have one who speaks in my defense, my Lord and Savior Jesus Christ. I ask Your Holy Spirit to help me, beginning right now, to enjoy victory over sin and remain in constant fellowship with You. But help me also, if I sin or fail, to immediately ask for Your forgiveness, set my mind right again and continue in Your presence, as if I had never deviated from it. In Jesus' name, amen.

The Rewards of
Vertical Living

26

Beauty Marks

*S*tay Slim Forever!"
"Killer Abs in Ten Days!"
"Five Steps to a Prettier Face"
"No More Bad Hair Days"
"Pump Up, Slim Down"
"100 Best Beauty Secrets"
"Eat More, Weigh Less"
"Megamodels: Their Secrets for Looking Good"
"Ten Great Summer Looks"
The newsstands and magazine racks overflow with such promises. Television and radio commercials claim that Oxy10 can clear your complexion, Miss Clairol can make your hair shine, and the right diet, right clothes and right foods can make you look like a model or movie star.

It's nice to be beautiful, but not all of us are born with perfectly placed beauty marks. But that's OK, because skin, hair and weight are not the only things that make a person attractive. The most effective thing, believe it or not, is holiness.

Of course, most people don't think of righteousness and holiness as being "attractive." That may be because their picture of righteousness involves a portly monk in a monastery or some spacey woman reciting Bible verses on a street corner. But true godliness—biblical holiness—is irresistibly attractive.

Look at the holiness of God the Father. Remember the story of Moses, who saw a burning bush in the desert? Moses approached the bush to see what was going on, and he heard a voice call his name and say, "Do not come any closer. . . . Take off your sandals, for the place where you are standing is holy ground" (Exodus 3:5). The holiness of God the Father was attractive, but inaccessible. Later, when God met Moses on Mt. Sinai, He warned, "Put limits for the people around the mountain and tell them, 'Be careful that you do not go up the mountain or touch the foot of it. Whoever touches the mountain shall surely be put to death'" (Exodus 19:12).

Bounds had to be set because God's holiness was attractive. He warned Moses to prevent the people from swarming the mountain of God— why? Because He knew they would be drawn by the beauty of His holiness. God's holiness was attractive, but it was also inaccessible.

Look at the holiness of God the Son. The holiness of Christ was God's holiness made accessible. It was holiness brought down to our level. It was holiness that we can see and understand. Jesus' holiness was apparent in His work, in His words, in His laughter and in His tears. And His holiness was attractive. The Bible says that "large crowds followed Him" (Matthew 8:1); children thronged him (Mark 10:13); men and women alike loved to be in His company. As far as we know, Jesus was not drop-dead gorgeous . . . but He was beautiful because He was holy.

Look at the holiness of God in us. The life of holiness bestows an unearthly beauty, an uncommon attractiveness on the young man or woman who "worship[s] the Lord in the beauty of holiness" (Psalm 29:2, KJV). If you've ever been around such a man or woman, you know what such beauty looks like. One man, an evangelist for many years, was not particularly dashing or handsome; but people stood in line to talk to him, to listen to him, to spend time with him at conferences, coffee breaks and luncheons, because they were attracted to him. The loveliness and natural beauty of a woman professor was magnified by her vertical lifestyle; young women in her classes tried (some consciously, some unconsciously) to talk like her, walk like her and dress like her. There were others, certainly, who were prettier than she was, but the beauty of holiness shone in her face *and* in her life, making her more attractive than Clairol or Oil of Olay could ever manage.

As C.S. Lewis, the author of the *Chronicles of Narnia* and *The Screwtape Letters*, once wrote in a letter to a friend, "How little people know who think that holiness is dull. When one meets the real thing . . . it is irresistible."

Word Up

- How much time each day do you think you spend working on your physical appearance (selecting clothes, combing your hair, etc.)?

  __less than five minutes
  __less than 10 minutes
  __less than a half hour
  __less than an hour
  __every waking moment

- How much time do you spend cultivating the beauty of holiness each day (in prayer, Bible reading, worship and fellowship, for example)?

  __less than five minutes
  __less than 10 minutes
  __less than a half hour
  __less than an hour
  __every waking moment

- Do you think you should change in either of the above areas? If so, in what way?

27

Dwayne's World

*H*ey, Barth, like do you know what time it is?"

"Like, I don't know, Dwayne, what time is it?"

"It's time for another one of *Dwayne's World*'s totally amazing, excellent discoveries." The host of the cable access television show tucks his long hair behind his ears and smiles at his co-host, Barth. "Our guest today has discovered, like, the secret to inner peace, dude. His name is Swami Yogi Andbubu. Welcome to our program, sir."

A robed, bearded man with wrinkled skin descends the steps and appears on camera as he takes his seat on the couch next to Barth. He cups his hands on his knees as if waiting for someone to pour M&Ms into them.

"Do I call you Swami or Yogi?"

Barth starts to snicker. "Watch out, Yogi, here comes the ranger," he whispers to the camera.

"You can call me Al," the man answers.

"So, Al," Dwayne says, exchanging a puzzled look with the camera, "how did you discover the secret of inner peace?"

"I have not looked on a woman for 47 years. I eat only what falls from the trees around my cave. When I am not eating or sleeping, I stare at the walls of my cave until I am at peace."

"And then what do you do?" Dwayne asks.

"I spend a lot of time watching reruns of *Gilligan's Island*. I have a satellite dish."

Dwayne and Barth stare at the man, until Dwayne slaps his knees with both hands and says, "OK . . . well, that's it for this week." He turns to his co-host and whispers, "Call the ranger, Barth; Yogi's escaped from Jellystone again." He faces the camera and smiles. "Until next time, good night!"

"Party on, Dwayne."

"Party on, Barth."

Dwayne and Barth apparently didn't find Yogi's story too convincing. No wonder. It *is* possible to experience deep and lasting peace in this life; it just doesn't happen the way Swami Yogi Andbubu said. It's one of the fruits of the vertical life.

Everyone who becomes a Christian experiences peace *with* God. As the apostle Paul said, "since we have been justified through faith, we have peace with God through our Lord Jesus Christ" (Romans 5:1). We who were once God's enemies (5:10) have been forgiven, and we have been saved from God's righteous wrath.

But it is vertical living that brings the peace *of* God. Isaiah addressed God with the words, "You will keep him in perfect peace, whose mind is stayed on You, because he trusts in You" (Isaiah 26:3, NKJV). That's the testimony of God's Word, yet how many Christians experience "perfect peace"?

Christian students still endure sleepless nights before their SAT or ACT tests, worrying over how well they will do, whether they will be embarrassed or disappointed by their scores and whether their scores will be high enough to get them into the college of their choice.

Christian girls wonder if the guys they like will ever ask them out, and guys worry that the girls they like will turn them down if they ever do summon the courage to ask.

Worst of all, some people—even after they have become Christians—still agonize about school, parents, friends, money and many other faceless, formless worries and fears about themselves and about the future. Their days are frantic, and their nights are fearful.

The promise of God is peace, but who can say they really know "perfect peace"? So few

Christians seem to experience the peace *of* God. That's because so few Christians have their mind "stayed" on God.

"You will keep him in perfect peace," Isaiah said to God, "whose mind is *stayed* on You, because he trusts in You" (26:3, NKJV). Vertical living supplies the ingredient that is so often missing from Christians' lives. Constant fellowship with God, through the Spirit, results in a deep and lasting peace that everyone longs for, but few experience.

This peace, "which transcends all understanding" (Philippians 4:7), is actually "the peace of Christ" (Colossians 3:15). Jesus said, "Peace I leave with you; *my* peace I give you" (John 14:27, emphasis added). Just as we have no holiness, but Christ "has become . . . our righteousness, holiness and redemption" (1 Corinthians 1:30), so "he himself is our peace" (Ephesians 2:14).

When a young man or woman begins living in the vertical, enjoying constant fellowship with God, Jesus Christ fills that person's mind and heart. While he or she trusts in Christ, and lets the Spirit of Christ rule inside, the result will be peace. As God promised through the prophet Isaiah, "The fruit of righteousness will be peace" (Isaiah 32:17).

Word Up

Take a few moments to think further about "the peace . . . which transcends all understanding" by completing the following:

- Are there any areas of your life in which you feel the need for "the peace of God"? Describe them below:

- According to the chapter above, how can the peace of Christ rule in your heart in those areas? What would it take? Read the following verses out loud to yourself, and then take a few moments to respond to God's Word in prayer.

  Romans 8:6
  Galatians 5:22
  Philippians 4:7
  Colossians 3:15
  1 Thessalonians 5:23
  2 Thessalonians 3:16

28

The Guys in Cellblock A

A cough erupted from the man on the stone
floor of the jail. He groaned and opened his
eyes. The cell was dark, and his feet were in
chains. He sat up slowly, moving carefully to
avoid reopening the bloody wounds on his back.

"Silas, my man!"

At the words of his friend and partner, Paul,
Silas remembered the events that had led him
to this dark, clammy prison cell. They had been
in the city of Philippi for several days when
Paul had cast a demon out of a young slave girl
whose masters used her as a fortuneteller, earn-
ing a lot of money from her condition. Once
the demon left her, of course, her masters were
a little peeved at Paul and Silas; they dragged
the two of them to court and charged them

with inciting a riot. They were sentenced to be flogged and imprisoned.

I must have blacked out while they were whipping me, Silas thought.

"Not exactly the Trump Tower, is it?" Paul said. Silas squinted through the dark cell and located his friend's form. Paul was also in leg chains, on the other side of the cell. Their shackled feet were separated by a yard or two of the cold stone floor. They could not reach each other.

Silas looked around him. The shadowy forms of other prisoners could be seen across the long room. He could hear the groans and complaints of others somewhere outside their inner cell.

"Oh, I don't know," Silas answered. "Have you tried calling room service?"

Silas heard Paul chuckle, then groan in pain. He could also hear a grimace behind Paul's voice when he asked, "Are you hurt much?"

"No, no. I just lost consciousness because I got bored, that's all . . . at least it wasn't as boring as your sermons."

Paul laughed, then cleared his throat. "Father Abraham had seven sons," he began to sing, "Seven sons had Father Abraham."

Silas joined him. "And they never laughed, and they never cried, all they did was go like this—ouch!" He groaned in pain as he tried to lift his left arm into the air. The singing stopped as they both started laughing. "Let's sing something else."

"OK, how about something by Amy Grant?"

"Yeah," Silas answered. "And after that we'll sing one of Carman's songs!"

Does that conversation between Paul and Silas seem unrealistic? After all, they had just been falsely accused, savagely whipped and unjustly imprisoned. Who in their right minds would try to sing praise to God under those conditions? Well, if you really want to know, read Acts 16:16-40, which describes the midnight praise concert of the two guys in Cellblock A (OK, so they didn't sing anything by Amy Grant or Carman . . . but they didn't speak English, either).

How could they act that way under such depressing circumstances? The answer is simple, really—they were living the vertical life and enjoying the fullness of joy that is the result (Psalm 16:11).

Living in the vertical does not guarantee that you will never know sorrow or grief, difficulties, disappointments or even times of depression; Jesus did say, "In this world you will have trouble" (John 16:33), but He also said, "Ask and you will receive, and your joy will be complete" (16:24).

One of the rewards of living in the vertical is a joy that transcends circumstances, a joy that "could not be beaten out of Paul and Silas with many stripes, but bubbled up and overflowed at the midnight hour in the dark dungeon, when their feet were in the stocks and their backs were bruised and torn."*

*(From *Heart Talks on Holiness*, by Samuel Logan Brengle, Salvationist Publishing and Supplies, London, 1897. p. 28)

If you are living in the vertical, "the joy of the LORD [will be] your strength" (Nehemiah 8:10) even when your boyfriend or girlfriend breaks up with you, even when your parents argue, even when your grandmother dies. You will not be immune from sadness or sorrow at such times, but the joy that comes from constant fellowship with God will remain in you (John 15:11) to strengthen you (Nehemiah 8:10), cheer you (Psalm 89:15, 16) and fill you (Romans 15:13).

The "joy given by the Holy Spirit" (1 Thessalonians 1:6) isn't like ketchup on liver; it doesn't just make your troubles and trials easier to swallow. It's more like a sudden rainstorm in a "dry and weary land where there is no water" (Psalm 63:1); it can start a praisefest in a prison, a celebration in a jail cell and plant a piece of heaven in a damp, dark dungeon.

Word Up

Some of the following "verses" are definitely *not* found in God's Word. See if you can identify the impostors and cross them out (check your answers by looking up the references in your Bible):

"Then will I go to the altar of God, to God, my **joy** and my delight." (Psalm 43:4)

"You became imitators of us and of the Lord; in spite of severe suffering, you welcomed the message with the **joy** given by the Holy Spirit." (1 Thessalonians 1:6)

"But there is no **joy** in Mudville—mighty Casey has struck out." (Psalm 151:12)

"But the fruit of the Spirit is love, **joy**, peace, patience, kindness, goodness, faithfulness." (Galatians 5:22)

"A thing of beauty is a **joy** forever." (Proverbs 12:35)

"Though you have not seen [Jesus Christ], you love him; and even though you do not see him now, you believe in him and are filled with an inexpressible and glorious **joy**." (1 Peter 1:8)

"I've got the **joy, joy, joy, joy** down in my heart." (1 Repetitions 1:7)

"I have told you this so that my **joy** may be in you and that your **joy** may be complete" (John 15:11).

- Pick one of the Scripture verses in the above list and meditate on it for a few moments in prayer, asking God to make the promise of the verse a reality in your life.

29

Holy Mackerel

"Today on *Okra!* we'll be talking to three peo-ple with the most incredible—some would say unbelievable—fish tales ever told."

The television talk show host smiles into the camera as the theme music plays through the studio speakers and the audience applauds en-thusiastically. Okra jogs down the aisle and mounts three steps to the stage, where a burly man with a heavy red beard sits uncomfortably in a straight-backed chair.

"Welcome to *Okra!*" she says, extending a hand.

The man nods and shakes her hand.

"Our guest today is Peter," she tells the audi-ence, "a man who claims that he was a partici-pant in a miraculous incident." She crosses her arms and faces him again. "Tell us about it."

"Oh, well, it was just one of many awesome things that happened in those days." He strokes his bushy beard with his crooked fingers. "About six or seven of us were out on my fishing boat on Kinnereth—"

"Kinnereth?" Okra asks.

"Uh, yeah, that's another name for the Sea of Galilee." He flashes an expression of apology at the host and continues. "Anyway, we'd been fishing about all night and hadn't caught much more 'n a cold, when we saw a guy tending a little fire along the shoreline. He waved to us and said, 'Caught anything?' We said 'no,' and He said, 'Throw your net on the right side of the boat and you will find some.'"

Okra stifles a yawn and nods at the man to continue.

"Well, see," Peter says, "that was kinda funny, because the fishing side of the boat was always the port."

"That's the left side?"

"That's right. But we did what the man said and dragged the net over the right side."

"Then what happened?"

"Just like that—" he snaps his fingers—"fish filled the net like aging hippies at a Grateful Dead concert. The net was so full we couldn't even pull it in. It was totally unbelievable; it was like every fish in the whole lake all of a sudden decided to jump into our net! That's when John—he was working beside me at the side of the ship—grabbed my arm and said, 'It's the Lord!' "

"Meaning who?" Okra asks.

"Meaning Jesus, the Christ, the Son of the Living God," Peter answers emphatically.

"What did you do then?" Okra asks.

"I threw my shirt on, jumped into the water and headed for shore, where Jesus waited." He smiles broadly. "We counted the fish; there were 153 large fish in that net—not a throw-away in the whole lot—the largest catch *I* ever saw. It's a miracle the net never broke."

"Holy mackerel!" Okra says, smiling for the camera. "Thank you for that fish tale, Peter. After these messages, we'll talk to our next guest, a man who claims to have proof that the Loch Ness monster has been kidnapped by aliens . . . next on *Okra!*"

Peter's story is more than an incredible fish tale; it's an illustration of the rewards that often come from vertical living. Of course, living in the vertical is no guarantee that you'll win the next fishing derby at the Lake Linda Fishing Club and Beauty Salon. But just as Jesus' words brought unexpected and abundant results that night by the Sea of Galilee, the vertical life can produce a new vitality and victory in a believer's life.

The vertical life enabled the apostle Paul to overcome shipwreck, disease, stoning and imprisonment to become the greatest evangelist and church planter the world has ever known.

The vertical life enabled Samuel Logan Brengle to survive the near-deadly effects of a brick that a rioter had thrown at his head, and enabled him not only to forgive his attacker, but to use his period of recovery to write the first of eight classics on the life of holiness. Brengle saved the weapon, explaining that if there had been no brick, there would have been no book.

The vertical life enabled A.B. Simpson to endure the disappointment of losing his pastorate at the 13th Street Presbyterian Church in New York without bitterness or resentment. It enabled him then to establish the New York Gospel Tabernacle, two rescue missions, a missionary magazine, a publishing company and bookstore, a missionary training institute, an orphanage and an organization that came to be known as The Christian and Missionary Alliance.

Among the rewards of the vertical life are the unexpected and abundant events that take place in the life of a Christian who is following Jesus every step of the way, who is tuned to His voice, attentive to His Word and sensitive to His will. The Lord can perform many great and mighty things through such a man or woman; he or she will prove the truth of Paul's words, "I can do everything through him who gives me strength" (Philippians 4:13).

Word Up

Take a few moments to confirm the message

of this chapter by completing the following:

- Read Romans 8:35-39. Verse 37 of that chapter says "we are *more* than conquerors through him who loved us" (emphasis added). Do you ever feel like more than a conqueror over the circumstances in your life?

  __Yes
  __No
  __Sometimes

- Have you ever experienced some unexpected and abundant results from your relationship with Jesus Christ? If so, what were they?

- Take a few moments to read through Romans 8:35-39 again, only this time use those verses as a pattern for prayer (for example, you might pray, "Father, I don't feel like 'more than a conqueror,' but Your Word says that I am. Let Your Son live His life in me, so that neither death nor life," etc.).

30

RAM, ROM and Ron

*L*ook at this!" Ron gripped a computer game box in both hands and showed it to his friend, Evan. The box bore a vividly illustrated cover and the title, *StrataWars*, in red-and-silver block letters.

"Yeah," said Evan, who knew more about computers than some software manufacturers. "That's a cool game."

Ron's eyes lit up like a toy robot on Christmas morning. "You have to find your way through, like, an underground maze, and fight off snakes and aliens and mythical animals!"

"Uh huh," Evan said.

"And then on level 87 you can find a StrataCraft and blast your way out of UnderEarth and conquer other planets and galaxies!"

Evan smiled patiently and nodded at his friend.

"And look, this sticker on the box says the graphics are like watching a movie in a theater! I'm gonna get this! How much is it?"

"Ron, you can't get that game," Evan said.

"What do you mean?" Ron turned the box on its side. "Look, it's only $69.95. I've got over $80 on me."

"I don't mean you can't afford it. I mean you can't run it."

"Huh?"

"You need a CD-ROM drive, 2.5 megs available RAM and a 256-color monitor. Your computer would take one look at that software and have a nervous breakdown."

Ron's eyes blinked rapidly, as though he were trying to clean dust out of his eyes. He looked at the box with the cool pictures on the front, and then looked back at Evan.

"I don't get it," he said.

Evan gingerly pried the box from Ron's grasp and returned it to its place on the shelf among games with names like *RotoCop* and *Dark Mansion*.

"My point exactly," Evan told his friend.

Poor Ron. He owned a computer, but he didn't understand that his system couldn't accommodate sophisticated software and games like *StrataWars*. His computer simply wasn't equipped to run such programs and graphics.

If he wished to play *StrataWars* or *Dark Mansion*, he would have to revamp his entire computer configuration, adding more RAM, more ROM, more razzle-dazzle.

In that respect, Ron's situation is a lot like the Christian who sincerely wants to serve God and to be used by Him. Take Sean, for instance. Sean is a 16-year-old Christian in a thriving church who wants to be more involved in his youth group and would even like to do some public speaking—you know, at youth retreats, outreach events, that kind of thing. But so far he's been paralyzed by "stage fright." He can't even bring himself to volunteer because he gets nervous just thinking about it.

Amanda is a college sophomore who became a Christian through one of the ministry groups on campus. She really wants to disciple other college kids the way her friend Angela taught her . . . but she lacks the confidence. She's afraid she would "blow it" and maybe make a mistake that would really hurt someone's faith.

Kashawna is a high school senior who's been active in her church's after-school program for two years. She loves the first- and second-graders she works with, but they get on her "last nerve" she says. She dreams of leading "her kids" to faith in Christ, but although the kids seem to love her, not one has ever accepted her invitation.

Sean, Amanda and Kashawna are all Christians, and they sincerely want to be used of

God. And each of them is serving God. But, just as more ROM and RAM would allow Ron to run the "cool" programs on his computer, the vertical life would better equip Sean, Amanda and Kashawna for spiritual service.

When the need arose to appoint people to take care of business matters for the growing church (Acts 6:1-7), the apostles didn't solicit resumes. They didn't look for people with college degrees or Wall Street experience; they looked for "seven men . . . known to be full of the Spirit and wisdom" (6:3). They wanted people with "vertical experience," not just business experience, because they knew that the vertical life equips an individual for service.

When the apostles Peter and John appeared before the Sanhedrin after Jesus' resurrection and ascension, they gave such an effective defense of the faith that the Sanhedrin (the same council that sentenced Jesus to death) was shocked; "When they saw the courage of Peter and John and realized that they were unschooled, ordinary men, they were astonished and they took note that these men had been with Jesus" (4:13). Peter and John had been in constant fellowship with Jesus Christ and that equipped them for effective service.

That's one of the rewards of vertical living. Oh, the vertical life doesn't guarantee that you'll never hit the wrong note when singing a solo, or that you'll never get butterflies when you're called upon to speak up for God, whether in a pulpit or in a college dorm room. The Spirit of Christ will, however, equip you and enable you to serve Him in ways—and with an effectiveness—you may never have dreamed possible. A young man or woman who has "been with Jesus," enjoying constant fellowship with Him, walking in harmony with Him, will be like a computer with *unlimited* ROM and RAM . . . and maybe even a little "razzle-dazzle."

Word Up

The following brief exercise may help you discover some new and important things about spiritual service. Take a few moments to thoughtfully answer these questions:

• Do you desire to serve God? Do you think He's leading you to serve Him in a particular way or ways? If so, what?

• Have you begun to serve Him in that way? If so, how effective do you think you've been?

• Would you like to be more effective? If so, how do you think you can accomplish that?

- Read Hebrews 9:14 and Ephesians 2:10. According to these verses, for what reason have you been cleansed from sin and created in Christ Jesus?

- Read First Peter 4:10-11. According to these verses, who supplies the strength necessary for effective service?

- Who should get the glory for effective service?

31

Holy Smokes

*L*adies and gentlemen!" The announcer wore black pants, a white shirt and a red bow tie. He paced back and forth in the middle of an area roped off like a boxing ring, surrounding two stone altars; atop each altar stood a stack of dry wood and large sections of a bull that had been slaughtered before the watching crowd. It looked like a Texas barbecue and Tough Man contest all rolled into one.

"In this corner," the man shouted, "wearing homespun clothes, the Prophet Elijah!"

Polite applause drifted through the crowd as the bearded prophet nodded unsmilingly.

"And in this corner, dee-rect from their successful engagement in Tyre, the prophets of Baal!"

Four hundred and fifty prophets of Baal strutted and danced around the ring to the cheers of the crowd until the announcer pleaded with them to return to their corner.

"Welcome to the Battle of the Century," the announcer shouted, "the prophets of Baal against the prophet of the Lord. Each side in the contest has prepared an altar of sacrifice. The prophets of Baal will implore their god, and Elijah will pray to his God and whoever answers by igniting the wood and consuming the sacrifice will be acknowledged as God by all."

The announcer called the contestants to the middle of the ring, repeated the rules, made them shake hands and then sent them back to their corners with the announcement that Elijah had generously allowed the prophets of Baal to go first.

The competition began. The prophets of Baal took turns praying and pleading, singing and shouting, dancing and drooling. Minutes stretched to hours, until they had struggled and sweated all morning, without results.

"Yo," Elijah finally shouted from his corner around noon. "You guys need to shout a little louder. Your god might be hard of hearing!"

A few giggles could be heard from the watching crowd.

"Maybe he's sleeping in today. Maybe he stayed up to watch David Letterman last night!"

The prophets began stomping and dancing faster and shouting louder, as the impatient crowd started laughing at Elijah's taunts.

"Too bad he doesn't have an answering machine!" Elijah jeered. He faced the crowd. "Yo, this is Baal. I'm not in right now, but if you'll stand on your head and howl like a banshee, I'll get back to you as soon as I can."

The crowd roared with laughter, and the prophets of Baal began to slash themselves with swords and spears to grab Baal's attention, but by evening, the stone altar remained unaffected by their crazed incantations. When the prophets of Baal collapsed, exhausted by their efforts and embarrassed by their failure, Elijah stood.

He strode to the altar he had built earlier. A large trench surrounded the altar. He spoke in a theatrical voice so everyone could hear.

"Fill four large jars with water," he commanded a few of the onlookers nearby, pausing for effect as the crowd waited in silence. "And pour the water on the offering and the wood." When the people had followed his instructions, he told them to do it again. When the altar, the wood and the offering had been doused a second time, he told them to do it again, until the water not only soaked into the wood and the offering, but filled the trench around the altar.

Then Elijah stepped a safe distance from the altar, turned to face it and began to pray loudly. "O LORD, God of Abraham, Isaac and Israel, let it be known today that you are God in Israel and that I am your servant and have done all these things at your command. Answer me, O LORD, answer me, so these people will know that you, O LORD, are God, and that you are turning their hearts back again" (1 Kings 18:36-37).

Suddenly, like lightning striking out of a sunny sky, the altar exploded in flames, driving some of the amazed spectators to their knees, and others face down in the dust. The sacrifice, the wood, even *the stones* were consumed in a breathtaking instant, and the water in the trench disappeared like a pinch of salt in a windstorm.

Even Elijah's eyes widened at the extraordinary sight, and he pivoted to face the crowd and saw that all the men, women and children on that broad hill lay flat on their faces, murmuring, "Oh, God! Please don't hurt me, please don't hurt me! I'll do anything you say. I'll even go to midweek service!"

Elijah's contest with the prophets of Baal on Mt. Carmel is a powerful example of answered prayer, but have you ever wondered how Elijah knew God would answer his prayer and consume the sacrifice? He was taking a huge chance, after all. What if he had prayed and nothing had happened? He was outnumbered 450 to one!

All those things were true, of course, but Elijah knew God. He was often called a "man of God." Elijah walked with God, just as Enoch had done before him (and, like Enoch, Elijah was transported to heaven without ever tasting death). Elijah called down fire from heaven not because he was a great prophet, but because God was a great God—and Elijah knew that because he lived a vertical life. That doesn't mean the prophet never knew opposition (he did; see First Kings 19:1-4). It doesn't mean he never got discouraged (he did; see 19:5-10). It doesn't mean he never made a mistake (he did; see 19:11-18). But it did mean that the vertical life—a life of dependence upon God and His righteousness—resulted in the power of God being displayed in Elijah's life.

That's another result of living in the vertical. When a young man or woman belongs totally to God and lives in constant, consecrated fellowship with Him, that life in the Spirit results in power—not the kind of power that magnifies the individual, but the kind of power that glorifies God. The kind of power that prompts bold, believing prayer and breathtaking *answers* to prayer. The kind of power that resists temptation and overcomes "*all* the power of the enemy" (Luke 10:19, emphasis added). The kind of power that conquers fear. The kind of power that courageously risks all for the gospel, that willingly faces affliction and opposition for the kingdom, that gladly suffers all for the cause of Christ.

"The eyes of the LORD range throughout the earth," the Bible says, "to strengthen those whose hearts are fully committed to him" (2 Chronicles 16:9). The woman or man whose heart is *fully* committed to God—who lives in the vertical, in moment-by-moment fellowship with God, trusting Him not only for salvation but for sanctification—may never call down "holy smoke" from heaven, but she or he will experience God's ability to do "immeasurably more than all we can ask or imagine, according to his power that is at work within us" (Ephesians 3:20).

Word Up

Confirm the message of this chapter by completing the following:

• Read through the following Scripture verses, underlining or highlighting the portion of the verse that says something about God's power (what He is able to do).

"Now to him who is able to establish you by my gospel and the proclamation of Jesus Christ, according to the revelation of the mystery hidden for long ages past. . . ." (Romans 16:25)

"And God is able to make all grace abound to you, so that in all things at all times, having all that you need, you will abound in every good work." (2 Corinthians 9:8)

"That is why I am suffering as I am. Yet I am not ashamed, because I know whom I have believed, and am convinced that he is able to guard what I have entrusted to him for that day." (2 Timothy 1:12)

"Because he himself suffered when he was tempted, he is able to help those who are being tempted." (Hebrews 2:18)

"Therefore he is able to save completely those who come to God through him, because he always lives to intercede for them." (Hebrews 7:25)

"To him who is able to keep you from falling and to present you before his glorious presence without fault and with great joy. . . ." (Jude 24)

- Is God's power to perform the above being displayed in your life? If so, take a few moments to speak a prayer of praise to Him now. If not, ask Him to show His power in your life in the area of your greatest need.

- Consider concluding with a prayer like the following:

  Father, I believe Your Word when it says that You are able to do immeasurably more than I could ask or even imagine. So I ask You right now to display Your power in my life, especially in this area: _____

  _____. Search me, and see if I have failed to surrender to You or obey You in any way and convict me of any sin. Lead me in the way of holiness as I commit myself to live a surrendered and sanctified life in the power of Your Spirit. In Jesus' name, amen.

- In the coming days and weeks, consider studying the many rewards of vertical living not covered in this book (for example, start with the fruit of the Spirit in Galatians 5:22-23). Most importantly, spend every day living in the vertical, and you will enjoy the abundant rewards of the vertical life.